THE NIGHT BUS BEFORE CHRISTMAS

J.A. BELFIELD

THE NIGHT BUS BEFORE CHRISTMAS

Published by J.A. Belfield

www.jabelfieldauthor.com

Copyright © 2022 Julie Anne Belfield

Cover art by Shower of Schmidt Designs

For everyone who ever gave me a chance …

CHAPTER 1

Morgan King stared into darkness. She didn't need to think hard to know she'd been asleep only a moment before. Just as she didn't need to check the clock on her bedside table to know it was far from time for any normal person to be waking up, but she did so anyway, lifting her head a fraction enough from the pillow to view the glowing digits.

01:11. In the morning.

Yesterday, it had been 01:13. The day before that 01:09.

Always the same time frame. Never earlier than 01:00 itself. Never later than 01:15.

As she always did, despite knowing it would never work, she forced herself to stay in place for another few minutes. Just in case.

Just in case she wasn't really awake.

Just in case she could fall back to sleep and rouse at a regular hour, like a regular gal, living a regular life.

Then, also as she always did, she threw back the covers on realising she had not a single chance of finding the oblivion she'd left behind, before slumping from the bedroom to perform her next learned step of the night:

Making herself a hot chocolate, in hopes that could succeed where her too-aware brain had not.

The ground floor apartment, which she'd occupied alone for the past two-ish years, felt as empty as it was, as Morgan stepped along the hallway past the bathroom. On her right emerged the lounge, looking almost as lived-in as it had since the day she moved in, nearly three years earlier. Back then, though, she'd had more than her own mess to navigate. Back then, it had been the beginning of an exciting journey that had ended far sooner than anyone could have predicted.

And, also back then, the space would already have been adorned in garlands and lights and a tree glistening with baubles and tinsel. Instead, all she had was a string of glowing flowers she hadn't even done a decent job of hanging around the window.

It wasn't that she had nothing else with which to dress the room. The Perspex box of decorations sat beside one arm of the sofa. The unopened tree box, still with its tatty tape bound around it from when she'd last packed it away, leaned into the corner of the room behind the armchair.

No, it was simply because .... Well, because it all seemed like too much effort for just herself. Too much effort for a person who left her apartment as early as she woke on Christmas morning, and sometimes didn't return for a couple of days, if her gran would allow it.

Morgan hadn't spent the past *two* Christmases at her own place, so really, what was the point?

Shaking away further images invading her mind, of shoes that used to be left askew beneath the coffee table, and music magazines that used to litter its surface above, Morgan opened the door to the small kitchen, flipped on the light, and crossed to the Tassimo in the corner. It took a minute, or so, of sleepy-eyed fiddling before the machine gurgled to life, and she leaned against the counter until it gave its final burp that let her know her steaming cup of cocoa was ready for consumption—enough time for her gaze to land on the calendar.

December 17th. Barely more than a week until The Big Day, as her gran called it.

Five weeks and three days since the anniversary of the worst night of her life.

Blinking wearily, as much against her obsessive thoughts as her fatigue, she turned away and retrieved her filled mug.

Steam spiralled before her as she passed back into the lounge, where she paused alongside a low bookcase. Picked up the small, framed photograph that always faltered her steps and demanded she stop and remember. Not that she needed the reminder. Morgan would never forget what she'd labelled snot-green eyes that'd always held such laughter—even more so at her refusal to change her description of them. Or the tiny quirk of his lips that seemed to sit at a just-so angle whenever he'd looked at her.

Letting out a sigh shifted the heaviness trying to climb on top of her chest. There had been a time when a sigh would've stood no chance against the heartache, but all those who'd told her the pain got easier with time had actually known what they were talking about. It hadn't gone. Maybe it never would. But it had eased.

Placing the picture back down, Morgan glanced toward the TV. Some nights, she resorted to that, but it never helped. Anyone who watched the screen in the early hours of the morning ended up either buying stuff their tired brain insisted they needed, or even wider awake from holding their eyes open on the brightness they should've been avoiding if they wanted to sleep. No, pointless shows and shopping channels would not fix Morgan's insomnia. She needed more.

As always, she'd just have to figure out what that was.

❧

01:59. For almost thirty minutes, Morgan had stood in the same spot in the spare bedroom, staring at the blank canvas like it might propose a way forward. Sometimes, the whiteness spoke to her, demanding to be filled with colour and movement, demanding she give it a story to tell. Other nights, it stayed as eerily quiet as Morgan's mind was screeching loud.

It was definitely one of the 'other' nights.

More whiteness surrounded her and the easel, too. On the walls. The ceiling. All of it spattered with a whole spectrum of colour, remnants of the nights she felt liberated from form painting and gentle strokes. From the nights where her passion spilled over from the canvas and into her life, strong enough to leave its gentle, yet vibrant, reminder of feeling uncaged. Even the hardwood floor beneath her feet held enough artwork of its own to house a gallery. Not that it mattered. Very few got to see the space she'd turned into her studio. Very few ever would.

Admitting to herself that she'd be adding no stories to those the room already told, Morgan set down the empty mug she'd been holding onto for too long, popped the laid-out paintbrushes back into the vase she used as a container, and left the room.

For a moment, she considered just going back to bed. Climbing beneath the covers. Ordering her brain back to sleep.

It wouldn't listen, though. It rarely did. So she took

herself to the bedroom to prepare for the only thing that worked when all else failed.

A glance out through the window showed slush-turned snow and a sky clear enough to suggest there might be more to arrive. Knowing it would be cold out there, Morgan slid her padded winter boots from beneath the bed, her thicker-denim jeans from the drawer, and her reindeer-patterned jumper from the back of a chair in the corner of the room. It took a few minutes to pull them all on over clean under-wear, another few to work a brush through her dark, unruly hair and a smaller one over her teeth. Aside from the pale skin staring back at her in the mirror, and the even paler circles framing her hazel eyes, she labelled herself fit for public appearances and headed out for her coat.

As she stuck one arm in the sleeve, she strode through to the kitchen, her steps more purposeful with her clear plan in place. She pulled open one cupboard, but closed it again on the tins inside. Pulled open a second and locked on the fresh bakery bag on the bottom shelf, which she drew out, before working her second arm into the padded jacket and pushing back into the lounge.

By the front door in the corner, a trio of pegs held a colourful array of headwear. On her way over, she scanned them all and decided on the turquoise bobble hat to go with her navy coat. Once she'd wiggled it over her waves, and checked her breast pocket for her bank card, Morgan opened her front door on the awful weather outside.

CHAPTER 2

A SOFT KIND OF QUIET GREETED MORGAN AS SHE CLOSED herself outside her flat. None of the usual bustle of the day. None of the tapping shoes and chatter and traffic and bright lights. Not unless she counted the decorations some of the neighbours liked to display twenty-four-seven, anyway.

The air smelled crisp and clear, and cold enough to assure more snow than that left underfoot would be along within the next few hours. Morgan already had to tread carefully, her body stiff in its battle against the cold. Thank goodness her boots had enough grip for even the local hills in the winter, or she might've been in trouble.

The journey to her destination was only a hundred yards, or so, from her place, but in even that short space, lights flashed out from windows, bright white icicles glowed out from where they hung beneath eaves. Across the street, the Brannagh house made her smile as she took in the deflated blobs laying over the lawn. Puddles of fabric by night. Giant snowmen by day, taking up over half the garden like something from *Ghostbusters*.

On her left, at the Peters', a light shone from the

bedroom. Likely not due to any nocturnal activity, but because their toddler, Jamie, still struggled with sleeping in the dark. It had always seemed a funny fear, to Morgan. Being terrified by something one couldn't even see. Or maybe it was just from not being able to see, at all. Even so, she didn't quite feel the need to be afraid of it, not when it was only temporary.

Real blindness, however ...

As she neared the local post box, Morgan trampled her way from the foot-flattened middle of the pavement to the higher, less trodden edge, as well as her nearest bus stop. However, standing there, her body emitting tiny shivers every few seconds, she worried the regular services mightn't be operating. That she'd made a mistake. Because what if the weather had laid them off? Who the hell would get her through the night then?

She worried for only a moment, though, before shaking the thought off. The bus had been running whenever she'd needed it last winter. And it had been running the winter before that, when she'd first discovered the much-needed reprieve to her newly-restless mind.

Four minutes of standing there, and Morgan had taken up a dance of stomping at the ground. Not because her feet were cold—her boots made sure of that—but because her bloody legs were freezing, and her fingertips were slowly turning to ice, because she'd forgotten to collect her damned gloves from the dresser before leaving, and the hand holding the bakery bag had lost most of its feeling. She'd thought she hadn't time to run back in for them, not with the bus due, but with it not having turned up yet, maybe she should have.

Again, she entertained the idea that the bus might not come at all, but before she'd fully formed the argument and convinced herself to give in, headlights rounded the road's bend farther down the street and brought with them the rumble of an engine.

"Thank god for that," she muttered, sweeping her icy fingers around the plastic card in her pocket.

By the time the bus pulled to a stop, letting out a hiss as its doors opened, Morgan could no longer feel her nose—or most of her face—for that matter, and she hoped the smile she wore as she stepped up into the warmth didn't carry the look of a woman turned demented.

"'Morning, George," she called, shifting to tap her payment card. "Here again."

"'Morning," a voice responded, sounding almost hesitant. A voice that most definitely didn't belong to …

Morgan whipped up her head and stared into the eyes of a stranger. "You're not George."

"I'm not, no."

She glanced down to his chest, but the driver's cab held too little light to see a name badge, if he even wore one. "Where's George?"

"Off. Are you staying? Or are you going?"

Morgan stared hard at him, unsure what to do. Every single night bus she'd caught over the past couple of years, George had, without fail, been behind the wheel. Lovely, lovely George, who'd noticed at a glance that all hadn't been right with her world the first time he'd seen her, despite his curmudgeonly demeanour. A true gentleman who had taken her under his wing and fed her the words she'd needed to hear, time after time after time, and who'd offered an ear accompanied by patience when she'd finally been ready to talk through her woes.

"I don't mean to be rude, but in case you didn't notice

yourself, I'm already running late because of this weather, so …"

Absently nodding, Morgan turned away from the scrutiny of the unfamiliar driver, but even though she fully intended doing a one-eighty and stepping back out into the frosty night, she found herself moving for the aisle.

A few feet in, the bus doors hissed closed, the engine gave a low rumble, and her body jostled side to side as she wound her way through the mostly empty, moving vehicle to the last low seat on the left.

She didn't know how, but that seat always seemed to be free. She'd chosen that one on her first night-time journey, and had continued to do so every other trip since. As if the universe simply *knew* when she would be coming and made sure her seat was reserved. She didn't know how she'd feel if she ever found someone else sitting there. What she'd do. Would she sit next to them? Find a new seat, maybe start a new ritual in a completely new position? Would her expeditions under cover of darkness be the same if she did?

She didn't know.

Sliding between the gap, she lowered her rear onto the rough fabric, shuffling herself over until her shoulder hit the window. From there, she could study the vehicle's other occupants.

Big guy, shoulders hunched—whether against the world, or against the cold, she couldn't be sure. Morgan had seen him before. A regular. One who kept to himself and spared nary a glance to any of the other passengers. Like he hadn't the energy or wherewithal to be arsed with small talk, or even mustering up a smile.

She knew how he felt. She, herself, had been that way. Before George had held out a virtual hand and helped her out of the lonely, dark hole.

Maybe someone should do the same for the big guy. Show him he didn't have to sit alone, armour up against the world. Someone who caught the same bus as him for more than three stops, as Morgan always did.

Like usual, a few minutes down the bus's journey, the man heaved himself to his feet as if it took all the effort he had in him, and lumbered from bar to bar, until he slumped a shoulder against the pole near the door. His body jerked and swayed with the motion of the bus, and he planted a foot out when the brakes sent him forward a step, the readied opening of the doors allowing a sound of wet sludge to roll in. As soon as the vehicle stopped, the guy barrelled outside into the cold, and as the journey continued, Morgan glanced over the few others left sitting, before shifting her attention to beyond the half-misted windows.

Back when she'd first caught the bus, she'd been antsy, unsettled, irritated by life and all it'd dared throw at her. She'd spent the entire journey wanting to be somewhere else without knowing where that somewhere might be. It had taken time for her to realise that it wasn't the bus she'd needed to be rid of, but her life as it was. The situation in which she'd found herself. The pain and turmoil, and the confusion over how to deal with it all. Emotions had a habit of doing that, though, didn't they? Slamming into a person with the force of a hurricane, before spinning them around and around until their minds no longer knew which way was up. Leaving them a dizzied mess in the middle of a mine-field they'd need to traverse before finding a safe ground upon which to function again.

Thankfully, Morgan's hurricane had been a fairly rapid one.

The minefield, though? Yeah, that'd taken quite the navigational hike to overcome.

Outside, the pavements stood quiet and still. A new snowfall had begun, tiny flurries of whiteness floating through the air to land on the greying sogginess the previous bout had become. Morgan wasn't surprised to see it coming down. The very air had smelled of the stuff.

Along main roads, questionably-shaped lights flashed brightly from lampposts, as if competing with those outlining peoples' homes. In comparison, very few lights shone from behind windows. But then very few people left their homes at such a ridiculous hour unless they had to, and thus had little reason to be up and about.

The bus jostled to a stop. One guy slipped out, as another moved in to take his place.

That'd been something she'd noticed early on in her nocturnal adventures. How few women ventured out under the shield of night. During the week, anyway. Sunday to Thursday, Morgan rarely saw another woman. In fact, she could count on one hand the number of times she hadn't been the only one over the past couple of years, and on those times, she'd received almost pleading smiles, as if the very sight of another woman aboard the bus offered enormous relief to the other female travellers.

Weekends, however, were another matter, entirely. Assuming, of course, she'd still to find solace by the time the last bus left from town. That was the bus all the clubbers piled into. Head's adorned with flashes and sparkles for the season, a detail lacking on any other night of the week. Youngsters and hipsters all loud and obnoxious with alcohol, yet filled with an energy Morgan almost envied. She'd never really cared for the party life. Never really gone dancing when all her friends had begged her to join them for a night on the town.

Back then, Morgan had already been drunk on the life

she'd been leading. Drunk on her creations. Drunk on warm evenings in the apartment, hot chocolate at the ready and enough marshmallows for a dozen people shared between only two.

Drunk on Philip.

She'd had everything she'd needed.

Until, suddenly, a piece of it had gone.

CHAPTER 3

FORTY-FIVE MINUTES OF GENTLE MOVEMENTS, LOUD HISSES, and intermittent blasts of cold later, Morgan's people-and-weather watching had almost come to a pause, with the signs directing traffic the right way to pass through the city centre. In daytime, vehicles slowed to an agonising crawl as they navigated any others trying to muscle into the bottle-neck of roads that narrowed more and more, the closer they got to the pedestrian zones. At night, the navigation held much less aggression with the lack of traffic about.

As she often did so close to the last stop, Morgan took a last look around at those who'd accompanied her on the trip. Tried conjuring up reasons why they might be travel-ling into the heart of the area at such an hour. Was it because they, like herself, couldn't sleep? Or did their reasoning hold far more purpose than her own?

She suspected it was, most probably, the latter.

Around the quieter than usual flow of traffic along the main bus route in, snow had begun a gradual gathering on the road outside. On the pavements, too. Morgan had always loved how the lamplight glow made it sparkle like diamonds, as if the world held secrets only the most perfect of environments could unleash for all to see. Loved how a night-time snowfall could bring light to the darkness. She felt privileged to witness it as untouched as it was, before the crowds would bustle in during the more sociable daylight hours and mar its perfection with their trampling feet, uncaring for little beyond their purchasing missions.

Overhead, the smaller decorations of passing towns had moved aside for the bigger, more flamboyant ones of the city. Candy cane garlands of tinsel hung over the road, threaded around streetlamps and zigzagged throughout. And hanging over pavements were huge gold-illuminated frames with messages of JOY! and NOEL! and REJOICE! alternated with outlines of angels and stars, trumpeters and bells.

The bus slowed to an even lesser speed than already adopted. Feet scuffed the floor as the gentle swish of move-ment surrounded the vehicle's interior. Morgan tore her gaze away from the wintriness of outside to watch the departing bodies trail down the centre aisle with as little enthusiasm as she had once felt for life.

One, then two, followed by three and four passengers disembarked into the cold, the bus dancing a gentle jive with each of them. Three long seconds passed, during which Morgan held her breath. After all, she only usually travelled with George. Kind and caring George, who would never dream of kicking her out into the night. She had no idea how the new driver would feel about company.

She finally exhaled at the heavy sigh of the doors clos-ing, allowed herself to relax back into her seat. Eyes on the driver's cabin, Morgan waited. Waited for his opinion on her being there. For his opinion of *her*.

Though, why she cared for that last one, she didn't know.

Maybe because a very real fear that George may never come back had ghosted through her mind, and if that happened?

Well, if that happened, she'd have to figure out a new routine. A new venture. A new way to exhaust herself when her brain wouldn't rest.

The lights of the bus went off, setting Morgan in more shadow than George usually placed the two of them. The engine died, leaving a peacefulness in its wake. She listened to the movement up front. Felt the stir of someone shifting about. And tensed once more when the driver's interior door clicked open.

A large silhouette appeared on the platform. Broad shoulders. Tall. Like he'd had to unfold himself from the confined space in which he'd been sat. Morgan saw slight movement, before the driver's door creaked shut. Heard a sigh, a sniff, fabric brushing against fabric. And then the driver began making his way down the aisle. Toward her.

In the dimmed interior, she watched his approach. Wondered where his gaze roamed. Did he study her as hard as she watched him?

A few more steps brought the driver alongside her seat, and she could take the silent scrutiny no longer.

"Thanks for not kicking me off," she said.

The driver jerked backward and fell into the seat opposite. "Jesus Christ!"

She reached out a hand as if to stop what'd already happened. "Sorry."

"You scared the bloody life out of me," he said.

"Sorry," she said again. "I thought you knew I was here."

"Maybe I would, if you were supposed to be here. But you're not."

"I know, but …"

"Come on." He pushed back to his feet. "I'll see you down to the door."

Morgan stared at his shadowed outline, unsure for a moment, before she admitted, "George always lets me stay on."

"Well … George *shouldn't* let you stay on."

"No, no, it's fine," she said, shifting across the bench toward him. "He says it's okay, so long as I stay out of the way, and—"

"Doesn't matter," the driver said. "You're not supposed to be here. Don't you have some place to be?"

"Yes." She nodded toward him. "Here. On the bus."

"Except, you can't—"

"Listen," she pleaded. "If you kick me off, all that will happen is I'll be standing out there freezing my cahoodles off, while waiting for you to finish your break and start your return journey."

"And then where will you go?" He sounded like he frowned, although Morgan hadn't a clue if he actually did.

"Well … then I'll get back on your bus."

Nothing. He probably stared at her like she was crazy. A debatable topic, she supposed.

"See?" she said. "That's why George just lets me stay on. He says it's not safe for me to be standing around the city centre in the middle of the night. He said—"

"Fine." He took a step back, and she caught the movement of his arms as he raised his hands. "But … just … no funny business, okay?"

She drew an *X* over her chest with her finger, hoping he could see. "Cross my heart."

"Sure," he muttered, before retreating back down the aisle.

A moment later, low lighting flickered down the front of the bus, casting just enough glow for Morgan to catch the apprehension on the driver's face when he turned back toward her. He didn't start back her way at first, seemed somehow hesitant about doing so. What he thought she might do, she didn't know. The guy was twice her breadth and had more than a foot of height over her five-two. If anyone should've been worried, surely that was herself?

As if finally reaching a decision, he quietly cleared his throat, then wandered back between the seats before pausing alongside hers.

"George and I usually sit at the back on his break," she told him, as if he'd asked the question.

Head tilted, he stared at her. With his back to the light source, shadows stole his expression, but that only made her want to see it all the more. His head started shaking. She wondered if he was about to refuse her, although she hadn't exactly asked him anything, had she? Instead, he lifted his palm a little.

"Fine," he muttered, before lumbering along the rest of the bus. "But we're not sharing a seat."

Morgan couldn't help smiling at her second small—or was that big—victory of the night, as she clutched hold of her paper bag and slid out into the aisle behind him. He really did take up a lot of room with his wide shoulders, even discounting the drooping rucksack hanging from one arm, yet he somehow managed to move with an easy grace his size belied.

At the back of the bus, he had to duck his head as he stepped up and swung to the right, where he slid his rear along the seat until, near the window, he faced the front. Complying with his stated term, Morgan climbed up to the left. She just didn't slide quite as far along the bench as he had. Assuming he'd even continue talking to her, she'd rather not have to be calling from opposing sides of the bus.

From the corner of her eye, she watched as he dumped his rucksack down on the rear-facing bench opposite him. The slide of the zip sounded loud in the quiet between them, as did the guy's rummaging around.

Allowing herself to look at him more fully, she held out her own bag. "Croissant?"

He quit delving and twisted toward her, but he didn't reach out, or speak.

"It's a thing," she said. "Between me and George." She tried for a smile, unsure if he would even see it, with how shadowed it was up back. "If I get the bus."

"What's *a thing?*" he finally asked—probably to stop her waffling.

"I bring a snack," she said.

He let out a sigh like he had no idea what to do with her and turned back to his bag search.

"I mean, I bring a snack to share with George," she said, a little deflated when he appeared to be ignoring her. "And George shares his drink with me."

"You want me to share my drink with you?" he asked, his movements stilling with his hand still deep inside his rucksack.

"Oh, I'm not saying you have to. I'm just saying … that's what George normally …" She shrugged.

"What if I don't have a drink?"

"Well, sometimes, George pops across to the all-night newsagents and grabs hot chocolates from the machine."

"Of all the buses," he muttered, as if he thought she couldn't hear him. From his profile, she knew he'd raised his face to the ceiling, could just see the movement of his muttering lips. When his head dropped back down, it faced her. "How many croissants do you have?"

CHAPTER 4

MORGAN SMILED. YET ANOTHER SMALL BARRIER BROKEN down. "Two," she said. "One each. If you want one, of course."

"Sure," he said, and despite the low grumble of his voice, Morgan decided she quite liked the sound of it.

She worked open the scrunched neck and held out the paper bag. "Help yourself."

The bag rustled with his acceptance of the offer, and with a quiet, "Thanks," he took the pastry straight to his mouth.

Morgan watched him for a second. The streetlamp outside the bus lined the edge of his jaw with light as he chewed. He had a strong jaw. Not jutting, nothing too prominent, but definitely strong.

"Why aren't you eating yours?" he asked, barely breaking between bites to speak, and Morgan jerked her hand into the bag, grabbed out her own croissant, and joined him in chewing her way through the buttery goodness. She'd barely gotten halfway through when he dusted his empty hands against each other.

"It was a good croissant," he said.

She nodded. "I get them from Sprinkles Of Joy. Corner of Chumbrey High Street?"

"I know the one. Never been there myself."

"You're missing out."

"So it seems." From his bag, he withdrew a flask, its metal flashing as it caught the light outside. For a moment, he stared down toward it in his hand, seemed to be contemplating if he should make an offer in return, before his face lifted toward her. "Did you …" He wiggled the flask in her direction.

"What have you got?" she asked, wiping crumbs from her mouth.

He seemed to grimace. "Green tea, I'm afraid."

"With honey?"

"Manuka, yeah."

She smiled. "I loved green tea with honey."

He shook his head, and what sounded like a low chuckle carried across the bench seat, making Morgan smile even wider. Another barrier booted, another small victory. How many could she wheedle her way through and over before her journey was through.

She watched as he poured the liquid into one of the flask's cups before twisting to hand it to her, and taking the hot drink, she breathed in the warmth and sweetness of it. "Thanks."

"Can I ask you something?" he said, pouring a second drink.

Morgan nodded. "Sure." Anything to keep him talking. Especially as he'd done so of his own accord.

"Why are you even catching the bus at this ridiculous hour."

Her shoulders stiffened slightly, a reaction she'd never been able to control.

"If you don't have somewhere you're actually going to, I mean?"

She let out a slow breath, nodding as if to encourage herself to continue. "I lost someone."

He paused in re-lidding the flask, his body seeming to tense as much as her own had. "I'm sorry."

"Thanks."

"Was it ... recent?"

"No, not recent." She gave a small shrug. "Not really. Just ..."

"It was a tough one to let go of." Not a question, but an understanding.

"Yeah."

"Must be hard, if it doesn't let you sleep."

"I sleep," she said. "Just a little bit unsociably."

"That's hard in itself."

She took a sip of her drink before agreeing with him.

He tapped the side of his plastic cup. "Too much time to think of a night, I guess. Less distractions."

"Actually, I think it's just that we had a routine, you know?"

"Routines are hard to break out of," he said.

"He worked the late shift," she said. "At a parcel sorting centre."

"Late hours are hard."

"They are," she agreed. "He started at six in the evening. Worked through until midnight. By the time he'd finished packing up there for night, and gotten himself home, it would be just past one."

"And what about you? Your work?"

"Oh, I work for myself," she said, waving him off. "But

I'd be in bed when he came home." Her lips curved, though she wasn't sure why. "And I'd wake every time. Right before he walked in the door."

"Like you knew he was there."

"Weird, right?"

"Sounds nice, not weird. You must have had a strong connection."

"We did."

"How long has it been since …"

"Just over two years now."

"And you're still waking up for him."

"Not for him. Not anymore, anyway. I think …" She cupped her drink, suddenly needing the warmth. "I kind of moved on from constant mourning a little while back. You know? I still miss him, but not to the extent that I can't get on. Or can't move on. I just …"

"Can't seem to stop the body clock from doing its thing."

"Yeah," she said, relieved that he 'got' it.

His shoulders hunched around his chest as he sat with his elbows resting on his knees, palms grasping his cup as if he needed warmth as much as she did. Though he hadn't looked at her once as she'd spilled her story, he leaned in toward her then. "But I still don't get why you're catching the bus in the middle of the night."

"Seems my body just loves routines," she said, letting out a small laugh. "A while ago, I caught the bus one night when I really couldn't get back to sleep. At least when Philip was still … you know. At least then, I fell back to sleep quite easily. Now?" She shook her head. "Anyway, I decided to go for a walk one night, and as I got to the bottom of my road, I saw the bus coming and figured *What the hell?*"

"And you've been getting the night bus ever since."

"Blame George."

"Why George?" he asked.

"Because he .... I don't know. He was *there* for me that first night I caught the bus. And I *really* needed someone to be there for me. I mean, obviously I have friends and family, but there's only so much they can listen to, and only so many times you can hear their same placations over and over again in the exact same tones as all the other times. Which makes me sound really ungrateful for them—"

"You just needed a fresh talking to from someone who didn't know him."

"Yes," she said, nodding. "Yes, you're right."

"George is your personal shrink." He said it deadpan, but she heard the humour in his voice.

"My shrink," she said, laughing. "He'd love that."

"Do you see your shrink every night? Is he expensive?"

"Around the cost of a pastry plus the bus fare," she said, grinning. "And not every night. Just when I can't find a distraction, or feel edgy, or .... I don't know. If I'm just *bored*, I guess."

"Ah, boredom. The destructive town in which negative thoughts are bred."

"See?" she said. "You know."

"Sadly, yes." He screwed his emptied cup onto the top of his flask, before looking to her. "Finished?"

She swigged down the last inch of her tea and handed him the cup. "Thanks."

"My break finishes in about two minutes," he said, as he fed the flask back into his rucksack.

"Does it really?" It'd gone really fast. Even faster than with George.

"'Fraid so. But ..." He clipped his bag shut and dragged

it onto his lap. "It's been nice having the company for a change."

With that, he hauled himself up off the seat and wove through the benches to the front of the bus.

Morgan watched his retreating back, trying to find something a little more discernible than what the dim lighting had given her during their talk. Just as he reached the driver's door, he turned back to her beneath the dull lamp and smiled. And oh, what a lovely smile he had, all tiny dimples at the corners of his lips, and crinkles at the edges of his warm eyes. After running a hand through chestnut brown hair, he pulled open his door and disappeared out of sight.

CHAPTER 5

FACE FROZEN FROM THE TOUCHDOWN OF TOO MANY snowflakes, Morgan let herself into her apartment. A little after two it had been when she'd left. Close to four by the time she returned. The small lamp in the corner of the living room seemed bright after the darkness of outside, and she squinted as she pulled the hat off her head by its bobble before unzipping her coat. Despite the padding she'd been convinced would protect her, pretty much every part of her body felt puckered.

With her top layers shredded, she moved through to the kitchen, but paused when she went for the Tassimo on the counter. Hot chocolate had been her immediate go-to, but something had her opening the cupboard instead. Had her reaching in for that long-forgotten box of green tea, and the jar of honey she mostly used only in baking, or when she felt under the weather.

The kettle bubbled its way to boiling while she prepared a mug. She tried to estimate in her head how much honey had been in the tea she'd drank earlier. It had been fairly sweet. Sweeter than she'd expected.

"Two," she muttered to herself, letting the golden stickiness dribble from the spoon into her mug.

Once she'd added the last scorching ingredient, she blew the steam from in front of her face and carried it with her into the spare room.

She half expected a repeat of earlier. Standing and staring at the undecorated surface while her drink went cold in her hands, but she'd barely even contemplated sipping from it before she set down her mug, picked out a paintbrush, and selected an array of colours. Onto her palette, she squirted out a blob of raw sienna, another of cerulean blue, a few others: titanium white, Payne's grey, burnt umber. Picking her tea back up in one hand and taking her brush in the other, she set about putting colour to canvas for the first time in weeks.

Stroke number one painted a line of greyed sienna across the screen, a combination of two colours that she roughly covered the entire canvas in, creating a rough, uneven coating of scratchy-looking grimness. The next colours, cerulean blue merged with a skinny streak of white, added a gorgeous contrast to that, bringing life into a room that often stood dormant for too long. It only took one more stroke of her brush, and Morgan was lost. Lost to the moment, and every moment that followed. Lost to the shade and dark of it all. But most of all, lost to the demands of her soul as she stripped herself bare enough to listen when it told her what to place where.

Hours later, almost panting from excitement and the exhaustion of having held her breath to get the perfect lines too often, she admitted exhaustion and placed down her brush.

From there, she headed for the bedroom, where she stripped herself of her remaining clothing, uncaring that she'd need to replace what had become paint-spattered items, and, finally, climbed beneath the covers ready for sleep.

"No! No, no, no!"

Morgan bolted up in bed. "Whah?"

"No," the voice said again, and after many blinks of her eyes, Morgan gradually focused on the burgundy chinos that were a little too short in the leg, the sockless feet tucked into loafers that were totally inappropriate for the weather, and upwards over the striped scarf that hung down between the open wool blazer clinging to the shoulders of her best friend Brandon.

"Ugh." She flopped back against the pillows and wrapped an arm over her eyes. "Do you have any idea what time it is?"

"Yes, honey, I do. And two in the afternoon is no time for snoozing."

"It is if you've had no sleep the night before."

"Partying?" She knew the optimism in his voice wouldn't be genuine, confirmed by the arch of his eyebrow when she dared peek from beneath her arm. "No, that's what I thought. You, darling, need to get a handle on your life and quit treating these midnight wanders like a drug you can't stay away from. Get up. I'm making drinks." He turned for the door. "And I'm certainly not waiting on your slovenly behind."

The bedroom still felt infused with his energy even after he'd bounced out and left her alone. With a grunt, she flung the covers from over her, her body instantly reacting to the chill of the apartment, though having flopped into bed in nothing but her undies couldn't have helped. A tatty robe clung to the chair, one she'd bought way before she'd even moved out of her gran's house. Funny how difficult it could be, letting go of favourite items. Like they brought a much-needed comfort in life with which very little could compete. With it slipped over her shoulders, she tied the belt about her waist, donned her slippers so her toes wouldn't drop off, and forced her weary head in search of the berating she probably had coming.

"Don't you ever use the heating in this place?" Brandon called from the kitchen.

"Yes, when I'm awake," she said, veering toward the thermostat by the door and twisting the dial.

"Except, when you are awake, you're either in a bloody trance, or out walking the streets like a lady of the night."

She leaned against the kitchen doorway, yawning as Brandon moved around her kitchen. "It's lovely to see you, by the way."

"It's lovely to see y—" As he looked across at her, his brows slammed down. "Oh, no, no, no." Shaking his head, he glided across to her. "No. Sorry, but *no*."

"What?" she asked, pushing up from the doorframe.

"Honey, you cannot keep walking around like *this*. How many times do I have to tell you?"

"What's wrong wi—"

"*Everything!*" Grabbing her shoulders, he spun her around and marched her into the living room.

"Oh, come on," she argued. "It's not like I'm going anywhere. Who am I going to see?"

"How many times do I have to tell you that the man of your dreams could come knocking on your door?"

She scoffed out a laugh. "Like that's going to happen."

"It could."

She twisted free to face him. "So, he's just going to be walking past the apartment one day and think, *Oh, hey, I know that place. It's the place where my perfect woman lives.* And he'll come strolling up the path and knock the door, and when I answer, he'll be like, *Oh, hi, I'm your perfect guy.* And we'll both live happily ever after." She let out a heavy sigh. "Life isn't a fairy tale, Brandon. I think we established that mine certainly isn't."

"You're missing my point, sweet cheeks."

Morgan rolled her eyes.

"My *point* ..." He drew her against his chest and wrapped his arms around her shoulders. "My point is that the guy for you could be anyone, anywhere. Who knows when he'll pop up. It's always when you least expect it, isn't that what they say?"

"Maybe I already had the guy for me," she said. "And I lost him."

"You're not ninety and just lost your husband of sixty years, honey. You're barely even thirty, and you and Philip weren't even together that long."

"That's a shitty way of putting it, Brandon."

"The whole situation *is* shitty, but life moves on and so should you."

Her chest rose high with the sigh she released. "So, you're saying I should always look lively just in case a nice guy speaks to me?" she mumbled into his scarf.

"It wouldn't hurt, hon. But what I actually want you to do is *look lively*, as you put it, for *yourself.*" With a hand on her shoulder, he turned them both until Morgan could see herself standing beside him in the mirror hanging on the wall. "What do you see?"

Morgan glanced over her reflection. The tatty robe she'd thrown on that had worn even worse since Philip had used to rib her about its condition. Her usually wavy hair all knotted and dry and brittle-ended. And eyes that stared out with little of the sparkle they'd once carried, from amid purpled and puffy flesh. "A woman who hasn't had much sleep," she said. "Because she hasn't."

"I see a woman who no longer gives a damn how she looks because she doesn't plan on spending time outside these walls."

"I do spent time outside these walls." She tried not to think of the driver from the night before. What he must have thought, assuming he even got a good look at her bubble coat and bobble hat and bleary-eyed stare. Tried not to agree in her head that Brandon might actually have a point.

"Buying cakes an hour before the bakery closes and catching buses when there'll be hardly anyone on them for you to actually meet and make friends with doesn't count. Catching buses when it's *not safe*, I add."

"I don't need to make friends. I have you."

"And I love you to pieces. But I'm not going to be enough for you for the rest of your life. It's time to expand your circle, babe."

"What if I don't want to?" she asked, pouting.

"I think, in this case, *need* trumps *want*." Still holding her shoulders, he guided her away from the mirror. "Go. Make yourself look decent. I'm treating you to a late lunch."

"From the bakery?"

"No, numpty. To actual proper food that you sit like a civilised person to eat."

"But—"

"Don't even think about finishing that sentence."

She huffed out a breath. "Fine," she said, and plodded off to her room.

"And, for God's sake, take a shower!" he called as she went.

❦

"WHO'S THIS?"

Emerging from the bedroom, Morgan paused at the open door to her art room and peered inside. "Who?"

Brandon glanced over his shoulder at her from his spot in front of her easel. "In the painting. It's good."

"What are you talking about?" Treading softly into the room, she took herself to stand alongside him and studied the piece she'd started in the dead of the night. "It's not a person."

"Of course it is. See? Eyes." He circled his finger in front of a few blobs of paint before waving it lower. "Nose. Lips. He's smiling, right?"

She vaguely shook her head as she tried to absorb the elements of the painting he seemed to be so clearly seeing. Elements that seemed to take form the more she allowed them to sink in. As much as what he'd suggested made sense, she didn't want to agree with him, though. "I don't know what you're talking about."

He peered sideways at her, as if he couldn't quite look away from the art before him. "You're kidding, right?" He turned to look at her more fully. "You're blushing."

"No, I'm not," she said, but she lifted her hands to cover cheeks that suddenly felt a lot warmer.

"You are totally blushing." He pulled her hands away. "Morgan King, you spill whatever story you're hiding. Right now."

"There isn't a story," she said, twisting herself free and escaping to the living room.

35

"Just like there isn't a guy in your painting."

She followed the sound of the kitchen door opening, and watched as he disappeared for a half-minute before pushing back through with a bottle in one hand and two glasses in the other.

"Lunch can wait," he said, flopping down onto the sofa and setting the glasses on the table. "This calls for wine."

Morgan didn't have the heart to tell him the bottle he'd found was virgin. Someone had once told her that alcohol inhibited sleep—unless one got completely annihilated, of course. She'd been drinking the lightweight stuff ever since. And Brandon had never noticed.

However, one thing she wouldn't get away with keeping from him was what had her blushing. Even if the whole reaction to a guy she'd met once—and briefly—did feel completely ridiculous to her. Brandon had no idea how to let go of bones, *or* any other analogies.

Twisting at the cap of the bottle, he met her eyes with his stern ones. "Don't wait for me. Talk."

With a sigh of resignation, she dropped onto the armchair. "Fine. There was a guy."

"Okay, *totally* wait for me. This calls for wine."

Morgan rubbed at the legs of her best jeans, while he poured a giant glug of the pee-coloured liquid into each of the glasses before straightening his posture.

"Proceed."

"It's nothing," she said, though the protest sounded weak, even to her own ears.

He cocked his head to the side and smiled in a way that wasn't really a smile. "Go on."

Huffing out a breath, she sank back into the seat, arms limp at her sides. "George wasn't driving last night."

"*George* George?"

She nodded.

"Blimey. You mean he actually has time off?"

"Apparently so."

"What did you do, then? Run away?"

"No, actually." She didn't tell him she was already on there before realising it hadn't been George. If she'd seen the stranger behind the wheel sooner …? Well, who was to say what she might've done?

"Is this story going to get exciting at any point?" Brandon grabbed up his glass and took a healthy swig. Morgan almost smiled at his wince of displeasure and the way he glowered at his drink before lowering it back to the table. "Otherwise, I'm going to think the guy you're painting is all in your head. Or worse—"

What he didn't finish but Morgan knew he'd been about to say was that the painting might be Philip. And it *would* be worse in Brandon's eyes, when she'd spent over a year convincing him she was on the right path to moving on.

"Maybe he *is* in my head," she said. "Something I just made up in the creativity of the moment."

Brandon stared at her, eyes narrowed like sights on a couple of missiles he aimed right at her deepest thoughts. "And maybe I'd believe you," he said slowly, "if you weren't blushing again."

Morgan lifted her hands to her cheeks, her palms instantly warmed by the heat there.

"Was it a passenger? One of them finally talked to you? Or, I know—" He bounced a little in his seat. "Someone *new* caught the bus."

"I already told you someone new was on the bus." Her hands slipped in to cover her mouth, her cheeks like an inferno as soon as the words left her, and Brandon smiled like he'd won a round of whatever they were playing.

"So, it was the *driver* .... Tell me more."

"There's nothing to tell."

"Your face says different."

Morgan slowly closed her eyes and puffed out her cheeks, but her lids flipped open again when something biffed her on the head, and she lifted her arms just in time to defend herself against a second swing of a cushion.

"*Tell me!*"

"You're being ridiculous," she insisted. "Last night's driver was different, and he seemed very nice."

"Did he kick you off the bus?" Brandon asked, lowering his weapon.

She shook her head.

"So, he let you stay on?" When she nodded, he continued, "Did he sit with you?"

She wobbled her head side to side, and Brandon seemed to take that as an affirmative.

"Did he talk to you, spend time with you, what did you talk about? Oh! What was his name?"

"Yes, and we didn't talk about much really. And I didn't get a chance to ask his name. He only had a short break."

"Sugar, people can make *a baby* in only a short break."

"Fine," she muttered, though she knew he wouldn't like her answer. "We mostly just talked about why I was catching a bus in the middle of the night."

Brandon fish-gawped at her. "I'm in awe at your ability to get the interest of a good-looking guy. He *was* good looking, wasn't he? Tell me he was good looking—no, scrap that. Tell me he was ugly, so your pathetic chat-up lines didn't get used on a hunk."

"You're so mean sometimes," she said. "And he was very pleasant looking, actually."

Brandon smiled. "You fancied him."

"Don't be ridiculous," she said, feeling her cheeks flame bright hot again.

"Oh, my little recluse." He pressed his hands together beneath his chin, his eyes ridiculously glossy for the situation. "You are finally *seeing* again."

She rolled her eyes. "I'm not blind and this isn't a miracle."

"*Mon chere*, you *were* blind. And this *is* a miracle."

"You're so dramatic."

"Thank you," he said, like she'd paid him a compliment. "But my gorgeous attributes aside, I think you need to get yourself back on that bus, honey."

Morgan frowned. "But … didn't you just lecture me on catching buses at night earlier?"

He flapped a hand toward her. "That was before you moved the goalposts and made the whole bizarreness more interesting. *And* before you started painting strange men." He pushed to his feet.

Morgan tried not to get stuck on whatever he'd seen on the canvas and sat up straighter again. "Where are you going?"

"Home."

"So, we're *not* having lunch."

"Oh, babe." He sighed. "You need more shuteye than you do food at the moment. Then you can flutter those lovely lashes at him without them looking like spiny grass over sand dunes."

Morgan blinked past the visual he'd created. "But … what if he never drives the night bus again?" It seemed the most plausible scenario to her. After all, she'd gone a little over two years of never meeting anyone but George, so what would the chances be?

Another two-point-something years passing before it

happened again, that was what.

"And what if he does?" Flinging his loosened scarf back around his neck, Brandon flounced in his usual way toward the door. He paused before opening it, twisted back toward her. "We are totally chatting tomorrow, sugar lump."

And with that, he was gone.

CHAPTER 6

01:03. THE NUMBERS GLOWED FROM THE BEDSIDE CLOCK bright enough to pierce Morgan's eyes.

She'd had nowhere near enough sleep since Brandon had left her. Thanks to him, she spent the best part of an hour staring at her work-in-progress and trying to create in her mind something other than the features of a handsome and gentle face. Then she'd spent the best part of another hour chewing at her thumbnail, while doing a terrible job of distracting herself with her copy of *Black Rabbit Hall*.

It had been early evening by the time she'd gone to bed. A small part of her had considered, just for a moment, setting an alarm to ensure she didn't sleep through the night. Because, goodness knew, she didn't want to listen to Brandon's disappointment if that happened. Nothing to do with the disappointment she might feel herself. But no, after little more than a cursory thought for the clock, she'd foregone setting it and climbed into bed and settled down, just as she did any other night of the week. After all, if she was meant to be at the bus stop at a ridiculous hour, and she was meant to catch the night bus on that particular night ... well, she'd wake for it all on her own, right?

And she had.

Lord, she really did drive herself mad sometimes. But to be fair, she hadn't had a very normal couple of days. Because ordinarily, her routine wouldn't have been altered. Ordinarily, she'd have bumped into George on the bus and moaned to him about not sleeping.

And that would've been it.

Instead, she'd met a stranger with warm eyes and a smile that didn't seem to want to leave her mind. A stranger who'd sat with her when he didn't have to, shared his drink with her when he didn't have to. *Listened* when he didn't have to.

And there was so much she hadn't got to tell the guy. About life. Herself.

About how scared she felt just knowing that, after what she'd been through, a man out there existed who could make her question her own thoughts in such a way.

Would she have confessed that, even if she'd had the chance, though? Could she have laid herself so bare and spilled such honesty?

God, why did she have to blow everything up into such a mushroom cloud?

He was *one guy*.

She'd met him only *once*, completely by chance.

And she'd spent a grand total of twenty-two minutes with him before he'd left her sitting at the back of that bus.

So, yes, pouring out her deepest fears and feelings would most definitely have been too heavy a topic for a chance meeting with someone she didn't even know. He'd have probably shifted about all uncomfortable with her openness. He'd probably have looked at her with relief at her depar-ture, rather than the smile he'd allowed. But then again ...

Balling her hands into fists, she squashed them into the dips of her eyes and let out a groan. Obsessing. Re-enacting. Obsessing again. Rewriting the script.

Did other folk fixate on circumstances it was too late to alter, like she did? Her gran said it was the downside of her creative mind. An over-imagination, she called.

Despite being all-too-aware of the fully-encircled looping of her brain, Morgan rewound yet again and wondered if the bus driver had been thinking about *her* since she'd stepped from the bus, as much as she'd been thinking about him, and inside her tummy, butterflies kicked up. Unbidden and uncontrolled, flitting about against the walls of her abdomen. She knew immediately what they represented. Excitement at having met a man who'd seeped inside her brain as much as Philip had the first time she'd met him. But, as always, travelling alongside that excitement, she also felt dread. Guilt. Fear. All for exactly the same reasons.

Lying there in the dark, her open curtains allowing branched shadows to dance across her ceiling, she reminded herself again. Tortured herself again.

You didn't even ask his name.

Knowing she would never, ever sleep while her mind rolled over everything so stupendously, she flung back the covers. And as she did so, she found herself caught on the what-ifs .

What if George had another night off?

What if he didn't?

She'd never know either way if she didn't at least lift her back from the mattress, and the way she saw it, she had two choices.

Get out of bed, or snuggle back down.

Try and find distraction at home, or … walk herself down to the bus stop in the freezing cold, and hope.

For what, though? For some company? Enlightenment? For the guy from last night's bus to be behind the wheel?

Having stood there a moment too long, the chill of the room sank into her skin, and the freshness of the air enveloped her in a way that awoke every inch of her body, working its way over her torso, until it'd seeped into her brain.

"*Blergh*," she muttered, swinging her legs over the edge of the mattress.

A thud hit the rug as she stood—her book from the evening before. Leaving it where it was, she plodded across the room, dragging up her tatty robe on route and slipping it over her shoulders.

The entire apartment held the iciness of a freezer as she made her way through to the kitchen and set up the Tassimo. Numbness spread into the soles of her feet from the chilly hard floor beneath them.

"Once upon a time," she mumbled sleepily, "there was a princess named Morgan …"

Beside her, the machine burped and gurgled.

"Walking through a forest of houses one day, she saw a handsome prince driving his trusty stead."

The Tassimo croaked its final sound, and she pushed her hip from the counter where she'd propped it.

"The end," she said, lifting her mug and taking a sip of the chocolatey goodness.

Bloody Brandon, she thought, not for the first time since he'd left her apartment.

Bloody Brandon and his idealistic notions, and his infinite optimism and positivity. Morgan already knew, if she walked out there through the darkness and planted herself in place for the bus to arrive, it would only be George back behind the wheel, anyway. Because one night of him being away could be considered a blip. More than that would mean something terrible had happened to the equilibrium of her life.

Or something good, she dared think.

"Not so good for George," she whispered. Because if George's absence *did* continue, that could only mean something had happened to him. And the very thought of that left Morgan cold. What if he'd gotten sick? What if he'd had an accident? Accidents happened all the time. She knew that first-hand.

What if he'd died.

Her fingers flew up to press against her lips. The very thought of something bad happening to the man who'd helped her to find the good in the world again was incomputable in her mind, and her heart kicked off into a rhythm of panic, but only for a moment before she gave herself a mental kick up the behind.

Thoughts like those? Maelstroms of negativity and despair? They were the exact reason she hated being alone *and awake* through the night. The very reason she'd found herself pacing the streets at an ungodly hour in search of distraction to begin with.

They were also what had her retracing her steps to her bedroom right then, where she found out clothes warm enough for the weather, before heading through to the bathroom for a quick wash and to brush her teeth.

UGH, who was she kidding?

Stomping her feet against the cold, Morgan stood in

snow that crept over the ankles of her winter boots, and beneath fresh snow that dusted over her shoulders and face, and wondered what on earth she'd been thinking. Why the heck she'd left the house with tiny flutterbies in her stomach and a ridiculous, unfounded hope in her heart. Just over the idea of seeing a certain someone for a second time.

A certain someone whose name she had no idea of, for which she probably should've asked.

The same someone who might've been to blame for her lack of rest.

As she'd stood at the front of the bus the previous early morning, waiting for it to brake at her stop, she couldn't help studying him out the corner of her eye. With a street-lamp sinking through the window from a different angle, she'd been able to see him slightly better and had drank in as many details as her brief stolen moment had allowed. The slight flick of hair that hung over the left side of his brow. The sharpness of his nose, but in a proud rather than pompous-looking way. A Roman nose, her gran would call it.

And then, when the bus had stopped and the doors had opened, he'd turned and almost caught her staring, but his smile had lit up any remaining darkness.

"Thanks for the company," he'd said.

"You're welcome," she'd told him and then stepped back out into the night.

You're welcome. Why the hell had she said that when there were a *host* of departing words she could've chosen instead?

I'm Morgan, by the way.

Maybe we could do this again sometime.

But no, just a simple *You're welcome.*

More than annoyance at her idiocy the night before, she felt irritated that she'd chosen that exact moment to begin stressing over it all. Why couldn't she have evaluated her poor social performance earlier? Or yesterday afternoon, even? Instead of about sixty seconds prior to the moment she might—or more likely not—be confronted with him again.

Just like the night before, coloured lights blinked out from properties and decorated the otherwise blank canvas of snow. Before her face, mists of breath curled through the air with every exhalation that left her. At least she'd remembered her gloves, and mindful of the flimsy bag she held, she banged her hands together, the thick fabric dulling the clapping to a quiet thud less likely to disturb the neighbours.

Just as she worried her toes might actually fall victim to frostbite, a low rumble of sound cut through the quiet, and she ceased to stomp and clap, and instead stared along the road toward the bend. She couldn't quite control the slap of her heartbeat, though, which suddenly seemed to drum against her sternum, growing more insistent the moment headlights appeared and the outline of the bus made its lumbering way toward her.

Her eyes couldn't have been any wider by the time the bus pulled to a stop and the doors hissed open, and not daring to look directly at the driver, she stepped up onto the platform with her usual, "Morning, George."

"Here again?" came the reply, and Morgan gradually lifted her gaze until it met with one of warmth and humour, and something else she couldn't quite decipher.

"I couldn't sleep." She shrugged, before adding, "Again."

"Well, get on, if you're getting on. You're letting all the cold in."

"Oh, sorry," she said, jerking forward to pay with her card.

Shaking his head like she'd amused, rather than annoyed, him, he gave a slight nod toward the seats. "Go on, then. Get yourself warm."

At the shuttering of doors, she almost jumped, before jolting toward the benches and the usual suspects on board. Big guy had claimed his usual seat, and would be leaving in a few minutes, as he always did. Other familiar faces, all where she always found them, too. And her seat, the one she took on every bus ride, empty and waiting for her.

Lowering herself onto the bench, she settled herself in for the ride.

As she watched the streets go by outside the window, Morgan could've been back on the last night's journey. The same decorations clinging to lampposts flashed past. The same lights across housefronts, and dead inflatables in gardens waiting to be resurrected. Classy white lanterns spiralling firs and small conifers in the centres of lawns.

One difference between the two journeys, however, was the number of swarms in Morgan's tummy. Like every insect with wings known to man had taken up residence inside there and swirled and danced right alongside her nerves. Nerves that seemed to heighten, the closer she got to the city centre. Because the city centre meant the driver would be taking his break. And taking his break meant that he might let her stay on again. Which would mean them sitting together at the back of the bus.

It was ridiculous, totally and utterly ridiculous, how jittery she felt over a guy she'd met once. And briefly, at that. Morgan couldn't remember feeling anxious to such a level. Not over a boy, or a guy, or man. Not even as a teenager at school, when her hormones had hit and every aspect of life got overexaggerated by default.

Possibly, although she hated entertaining the idea, not even with Philip?

Sighing, she stared toward the front of the bus, partially irritated with herself for the notion she'd dared ponder. Even so, for a moment, she wondered how often the driver checked his rear-view mirror. Entertained the idea that he might be looking toward her, as she looked toward him.

What did that tell her, that thoughts of the man she'd met only twenty-four hours earlier could push out the thoughts that had so consumed her for the past few years?

Then she berated herself again for being so ... *immature* over a guy. She should have been taking a more reserved route. Laying back and taking it easy. Well, maybe not *laying back*, exactly, but definitely, she should've thought it over more. Like whether, or not, she should be on the bloody bus, at all, considering it was the first interest she'd shown in *anyone* since Philip's death. Or the first interest her body seemed to have shown, anyway.

It had been a long time since Morgan's nerve endings had felt quite so *buzzy*. And a part of her, a big part, wanted to run screaming for the covers of her bed and hide, hide away from that for a very long time.

CHAPTER 7

FAR TOO LONG AND FAR TOO SOON LATER, THE BUS HISSED open its doors for the final time in its current direction, and the vehicle jostled with each disembarking passenger. Chilled air seeped in around their bodies, somehow managing to snake the length of the aisle and wrap its tentacles around Morgan on passing. She shivered in her seat, and then convinced herself it had been *only* the cold that'd caused it. Absolutely nought to do with the fact that she'd be sat in the shadowed rear of the bus very soon with a man about whom she knew very little.

Hopefully, anyway.

Just as she had during the previous trip she'd taken, she held her breath as the last of the passengers left and the doors cranked then clapped shut. Held her breath as nary a sound accompanied the movement she sensed from the driver's cubby ahead.

A whole minute seemed to pass before a click warned her the door was about to open, and as it swung outward, the large body she'd been thinking about for almost twenty-four hours pushed its way free.

The guy closed the door on his quarters, before giving a quiet huff as he slung his backpack over one shoulder. His face lifted then, and Morgan had to wonder if he sought her out through the darkness. Wondered how much of her face he could actually see.

Wondered *what* he might see.

Anticipation? Nerves? All the other emotions she felt far too terrified of to explore?

Possibly all of the above.

After what seemed like the briefest of hesitations, he rolled his way along the aisle until he reached where she sat waiting.

"You're still here, then?" he asked through the shade.

"Where else would I be?"

"I would say *in bed*." Humour laced his tone. "But bed at night is for normal people ..."

"I'm afraid I don't fall into that category," she said, her fingers almost twisting a knot into the bakery bag as he breathed out what sounded like a quiet laugh.

"Come on, then."

Without further words, he lumbered on past her toward the rear of the bus.

For a moment, Morgan stayed where she was. He hadn't kicked her off—again. But he hadn't exactly sounded exalted at her company for a second shift, either.

Although, she had seemed to amuse him. Maybe.

Or maybe not.

Either way, she'd never find out if she didn't move her arse from its current position, so she drew herself to her feet and slipped out from between the seats until standing in the aisle. The trouble with buses, though, whether they rolled along, or didn't, was that it was very difficult to move through them with any kind of elegance. The width of the aisle never quite permitted a full-front-facing glide. And swinging one's hips side-to-side with the necessary exaggeration to get from one point to another always made Morgan feel as though she resembled a deranged belly dancer.

At the back of the bus, she found the driver in the same spot he'd taken the last time, and in replication of the event, she stepped up to her left and twisted herself onto the raised rear bench. Once there, though, she had little idea what she should do, and after a few brief seconds of scrunching the neck of the paper bag she held, she found her head twisting toward the opposite corner. From where, she quickly realised, the guy stared her way.

"What did you bring tonight?" he asked, nodding toward the crinkling she created.

She held it up, like he hadn't already seen it. "Chocolate muffins?" she said it like a question with little idea as to why.

"Somebody tell you I have a sweet tooth, did they?"

"No." She frowned down at the bag for a moment, then glanced his way again. She seemed braver with looking at him since the previous night. "Do you?" Braver with the more direct questions, too.

"It's why I drink green tea."

"Green tea isn't sweet," she said. Not unless he counted the honey he liked to add.

"No, but it certainly makes me feel better about eating the sweet stuff."

Morgan gave a quiet laugh. "A good choice counteraction against the bad?"

"You've got it."

"I like how you think," she said, staring a little harder through the gloom. For some reason, although his tone of voice told her plenty, she needed to know for sure that he smiled. He sounded like he did, but she wanted to *see*.

Or maybe she merely wanted to see his smile again, whatever the circumstances.

"So, do I get one?" he asked.

She jumped slightly, gave an upward snatch of the bag. "Of course you do." She nigh on thrust the rustled paper toward him, barely remembering to release where she squeezed its neck when he took it from her hands and reached in for his offering.

"Looks good," he said, handing the remaining muffin back to Morgan.

"It should—it's from Sprinkles Of Joy." She could have groaned at her idiotic response. He'd probably figured that out on his own—if not from her comment the night before, because she shouldn't assume he'd actually remembered their conversation, then from the printed lettering on the side of the bag.

"Well, if it's as good as the croissant …"

"It will be," she assured him.

"Maybe I'll have to give this place a visit of my own. Is it near to you—where you live?"

Obviously, Morgan's twisted mind had to try over-assessing the question. Did he want to know because he was interested in her? Or because he really wanted to visit the bakery?

But he'd said he knew the place, hadn't he? When she'd mentioned it on the last journey she took?

"Sorry," he said into the prolonged quiet. "You don't have to answer that."

"It's not far." She could've kicked herself. Spending more time inside her head than out, wasn't that something Brandon always accused her of? Maybe he had a point. "Takes about ten minutes, that's all."

"I only know the area at all because of the buses," he

said.

Morgan blinked. Had he just offered up a personal dot of information about himself? Obviously, she jumped right on that. "You're not from around here, then?"

He shook his head, and she couldn't help but notice how he sat a little straighter than he had previously. On first meeting him, he'd been hunched—almost closed off. Beside her right then, he didn't seem to have quite as heavy a shutter in place to block her out. "I live over Wellsdon way."

She watched his profile bite off a hunk of muffin and chew, as she tried to place the name of the town he'd offered up, but she had no bloody idea where it was.

Almost as if he knew she watched, he turned to her, and almost as if he could hear the well-oiled, if somewhat worn, cogs of her brain overworking, he pointed in a way that wasn't really any indication of a direction. "Other side of Sutton-On-Down. It's a village more than town. Probably why you've never heard of it." He looked back down toward the cake he held. "Most folk haven't." He took another bite and chewed.

"Aren't blokes from villages usually farmers?" she asked.

An almost-loud bark of laughter flew from him, hard enough that Morgan jumped in her seat, before grinning like an idiot at the achievement. "Yeah, I guess they are," he said, his tone a smidgeon higher in his amusement.

"But not you?"

He peered over for a half beat, before rummaging in his rucksack and drawing out his flask. "Nah, not me."

She watched as he poured out two cups, the sweetness of honey the dominant scent in the steam floating from the one he passed over to her. "Cows and cabbages not really your thing, then?"

"I dunno." His entire body seemed to move with his shrug. "I guess I've never really known what's my thing."

"So, you didn't wake up one day and decide you just *had* to be a bus driver?"

Another laugh, though nowhere near as monumental as the first. "Who really knows what they want to be? What they want to do? Isn't that what life is—us all wandering around blindly trying to figure it all out, and then ..."

And then, what? she wanted to ask. *We all die?* Instead, she told him, "I knew. I always knew."

"What you wanted to do?"

"Yes."

"Right. But most times, we never actually get to be what it is we *think* we want to be. Or we get there and it's nothing like we expected. You know?"

"Life *isn't* anything like I expected, but it has nothing to do with my job."

He sat up straighter, turned more fully toward her. "You sound like you're defending your job."

"I am."

"Which means you must like it—or it's so corrupt, you need to justify it."

Morgan laughed. "It's not corrupt. That's the most ridiculous thing I've ever heard."

"Okay, I'll bite." He sounded like he smiled. "What is it you do?"

"I'm an artist," she said simply.

"As in, paints and paintbrushes and knotted hair and dungarees?"

"That's an interesting image you have of an artist, but yes."

"And you actually make enough money to live off from it?"

"I don't usually discuss money with people, but as you didn't sound like a condescending arse when you asked ... yes. Yes, I do."

He didn't look away. He didn't speak. Morgan had rarely felt so scrutinised, and definitely not by someone she could barely see and who made her feel as though her flesh was heating up beneath her clothing, and she suddenly needed to look everywhere but at him.

"You're lucky," he eventually said into the quiet.

Lucky? Morgan couldn't remember ever addressing herself with the word, and certainly not in the past couple of years, but the way he'd made her feel studied, the way he'd said those two words, almost as if filled with reverence more than envy, forced her to consider the point. "I guess I am," she finally admitted.

CHAPTER 8

MORGAN SPENT THE ENTIRE RETURN JOURNEY HOME evaluating the words shared by the driver. And even more evaluating her agreement with them. Because she *was* lucky. She knew that—deep down, she truly did. Sometimes, though, life just got so heavy that one spent all of their energy scrabbling with the sheer weight of it all, leaving them with so little left to take a step back and remember what they had to feel thankful for.

Had that been her own recent path? Had she truly been so busy lamenting that she'd forgotten to appreciate? Forgotten *how* to, even?

She appreciated George, though, didn't she? And she appreciated Gran and Brandon and everyone else who tugged on her strings whenever it felt as though they'd been snipped?

What about everything else, though? That she could still work from home—still take a day off whenever she didn't feel up to creating—could still create even on her darkest of days if the muse grabbed hold of her misery and turned it into something spectacular? Why didn't she feel appreciative enough of the fact that she supported *herself*, damn it?

Why didn't Morgan ever simply feel thankful for Morgan?

Barely registering the passing streets beyond the windows, she looked up in surprise when the bus drew to a halt and the driver poked his head out of the door.

"This is you, right?" he called down the bus.

It was a gesture she received often from George, but for some reason, when prompted by the words of a man she knew so little about, the scrutiny she received from the smattering of passengers felt much more intrusive than it usually did.

Forcing herself not to shrink into her seat, she craned her head out into the aisle. "I'll get off on the way back, if that's okay?"

He somehow twisted further in the small space he occupied, until she could see most of his face and two tiny shining spots of light on eyes she just knew he aimed her way. One second, two, three seconds passed, and she could have sworn he smiled before ducking back into his hidey hole and rumbling along the road once more.

With a smile ghosting her own lips, Morgan retreated back into her seat and inside her chaotic mind, and settled in for the ride.

THE RIDE to the journey's end in the other direction always seemed to take much longer. Morgan *told* herself it always did, anyway. That the lengthier stretching of time had little to do with anticipation. Except, the way he'd spoken to her earlier seemed filled with so much more ease than the previous night's chat. *He'd* been so much more at ease. And a large part of Morgan needed to explore than further.

Or maybe she merely wanted to explore *him*.

For the first trip in a long while, Morgan took little notice of the other passengers climbing aboard before disembarking. She paid little mind to the flashing of lights they passed, other than to acknowledge the invasion into her vision. Instead, she relaxed against her seat and the carriage wall and loosed her mind of restraint, until she conjured up fields surrounding the village where he might live, and scenery of cows and hedgerows and quaint little cottages, and people all waving hello with the kind of familiarity that came from living somewhere like that. She thought of kind eyes and small flicks of hair, and the painting standing on her easel at home, and how much more she needed to add to get it *just right*.

Not to make it more like the driver, though. She was still in far too much denial over that. She just knew something within the glisten on the subject's eyes needed a slight tweak, and that it had little to do with the way she'd felt *him* look at her before continuing on the route. It couldn't have, not when she'd barely been able to see his expression. Right?

More snow drifted past the windows as they rolled through the streets at the far end of the journey. Not a city, but a town. And not at a terminal but on a regular road that met another in a T-junction, but where the buses parked up to the side as if in refusal to roll even an inch farther. No bus stop at that point, either. The last passenger had stepped into the cold a hundred yards back, so as the driver rolled up against the kerb and the engine coughed its way to quietness, only Morgan sat in the bus proper.

As she had the past couple of times, she tensed. Watched. Waited. She could hear switches being flicked, and the sweeping of fabric, and even felt his movements through the slight sway of the vehicle.

The driver door clicked then swung open, and his large form stepped out, seemed to unfold from itself, until he stood at full height and impressive breadth, and the sigh he released carried the length of the aisle.

"You mind if I leave the light off here?" he asked without moving.

Frowning, Morgan glanced around her. There was enough lamplight from outside to see by, she supposed. "Okay?"

"It's just … this place is kinda creepy at night."

"Creepy?" she asked.

"Yeah." He closed his door and started along the bus's length. "It might be in a town, but it's like it's in the middle of nowhere."

Morgan peered out of the windows. A couple of shadowed football pitches surrounded by trees on one side. A park on the other, abandoned beneath the night sky and barely recognisable for what it was with the darkness cast across it.

"And then every so often kids or young guys come past like they've nowhere better to be and …" He stopped alongside her. "Well, let's just say, I don't particularly want to be subjected to them banging on the windows and yelling just because they've spotted someone in here."

She blinked. "Does that happen a lot?"

"Once. Which is once too many." He jerked his head. "'Coming?"

"Yes," she said simply, and as he lumbered the rest of the way to the back, she slipped from her seat and followed.

CHAPTER 9

THE DRIVER HAD BEEN QUIET FOR TOO LONG. AND WITH only one muffin left, she wasn't sure what to lead in with to get him to talk again.

God, why did everything have to be so *hard?*

She'd mostly hoped he would just continue on their chatter from earlier. At least make it easier for her than he was. Instead, he sat hunched slightly, his shoulders rounded, his hands hugging the plastic cup from his flask. He hadn't even poured one for her.

A short way from the houses of the area, very little noise beyond their own broke into their shared space. With it being a town, very little wildlife, even, disturbed the quiet.

Wringing the neck of the paper bag, Morgan glanced sideways at him. She could see very little of his expression, but he didn't seem to be looking at anything in particular, more lost in thought. "Is everything okay?" she ventured.

He jumped slightly, as though her speaking had startled him, before he breathed out a quiet laugh and twisted to face her. "Sorry, I was miles away then." He passed over the cup in his hands like he'd every intention of doing so all along.

"Penny for them," she said, taking the offered drink.

"You sound like my mum." He set down the other plastic mug, began pouring a second serving of tea, and Morgan watched him, unsure how to respond to the observation.

"Is that an insult, or a compliment?" she asked, trying to inflect humour into her tone.

He twisted toward her again, leaned in almost close enough to bump his shoulder with hers. "Not an insult."

"That's good to hear," she said, suddenly aware of how much closer to her he'd sat. He hadn't shuffled all the way to the window. Hadn't insisted she not sit beside him. "Men who use their mother as an insult aren't usually very nice men," she added.

"Yeah, I guess they aren't." He nodded along with his words, but as the action died down, so, too, did his spurt of enthusiasm. His shoulders hunched back in again. His head seemed to hang a little lower from the end of his neck.

"Really, though," Morgan said, before any awkward silences could recommence. "*Are* you okay?"

More nodding, but only a half-hearted effort, really, before he stilled. From his profile, he seemed to be staring straight ahead, once more as if seeing something in his mind, or lost in thought. "It's just this time of year, I guess."

She fish-mouthed for a moment, then asked, "Christmas?"

"More December."

"You don't like December? Because, really, December is a fairly large chunk of the year, if you do the maths ..."

She'd hoped for a smile, at least, but she got nothing, and he didn't speak for at least half a second, before:

"Mostly just around the seventeenth." He glanced her way. "It's a hard date for me, you know?"

Morgan *did* know. All too well. "Did something happen on the seventeenth?"

His head did that action again, like he tried nodding but hadn't quite the stamina for it. "I lost someone."

"Oh. I …" Morgan hadn't been expecting those words, but really why shouldn't she have? She didn't have a copyright on losing someone important. Didn't have the claim to being left alone by a significant other. Forcing her mind away from herself and the sudden surge of panic welling inside her, she reached out and touched his arm. "I'm sorry."

He half-peered at her. "Thanks."

"Has it …" God, she didn't even know the etiquette for this kind of talk—and she should have, damn it. She should have known the right questions to ask inside-out. "When …?" Was this how all of her family and friends had felt around her? Scared and panicked and terrified of saying, or asking, the wrong thing? "Has it been very long since …?"

"Last year."

"God, I'm sorry." A year was no time at all. "And there was me waffling on about my own troubles last night—"

He gripped her hand, gave it a gentle shake. "Hey, don't be sorry. A person shouldn't ever be sorry for needing to talk."

"Thank you," she said, breathing out a sigh.

"If we can't talk to others, what do we have?"

She thought of herself, the way she preferred closing herself indoors and retreating into her own mind. Even as she'd done it—every time she'd done it—she'd known it wasn't a healthy situation in which to place herself. Could acknowledge how much better she felt whenever Brandon

forced her woes from her and kicked her arse into shape.
"Very little," she admitted to the driver, which was why she
added, "If you needed to talk now ..."

He took a sip of his cooling drink. "Thanks. Mostly, I'm
okay. I think it's just ..."

"The anniversary is coming up."

"Yeah."

"Sorry, but I have to ask ..." She needed to know. "Did I
make this harder for you—"

"Nah." He straightened in his seat, head shaking as he
angled his head toward her. "Nothing to do with you. It
would be hard anyway."

"You're sure."

He patted her hand where it still half rested against his
arm. "Positive."

"Good." She finally let her hand drift away, but not too
far that she couldn't reach out again if she felt he might
need it. "You know, you could talk to me, if you needed.
Goodness knows, I dumped enough of my problems on you.
Seems only fair you get a go."

A small chuckle accompanied his exhale, and Morgan
couldn't help but smile at the win. She seemed to be earning
a good few of them since meeting the driver, even if she did
have to work for the prize.

"I'm guessing you were close to them?" she prompted.

He peered over. "About as close as I've ever been to
anyone who's not in my immediate family."

She swallowed as she contemplated his words. Tried not
to acknowledge the knot in her throat, because she didn't
care that it sounded as though he'd had a relationship with
his passed 'someone'. She had no right to feel stung by that,
considering her own situation.

Or maybe she felt disappointed that he'd lost someone

so important to him so much more recently than herself, and if her own experience was anything to go by, it could be a long, long time before he might be up for anything new.

Anything new?

Pargh!

Like Morgan even knew what that meant, herself. Like she even knew what *she* wanted.

"What was their name?" she asked, ordering her own warbling mind to quiet.

"Luke."

The moisture about dried up in her throat. Luke? That made his 'someone' a *guy*! Not for one moment had Morgan contemplated the idea that the driver might prefer men.

Ordering her panic to sit on the back burner, she forced out, "What was he like?"

"He was my best friend."

Just like her and Philip.

"We did everything together."

So had she and Philip, whenever they hadn't been working.

"It's just this bloody guilt, you know?"

Guilt? Everyone had gone on about it to her, too. Almost convinced her she was *supposed* to be feeling it. But she hadn't felt *guilty*. Devastated, for sure, but not that.

"I feel like that's all I've been carrying around with me this past year."

"Survivor's guilt, they call it," she said, suddenly remembering.

He frowned, pausing for a moment before saying, "This has nothing to do with me surviving. This is because I should have done more when I could."

"Oh! I'm sorry. Did he …?" Good Lord, had he killed

himself? What an oaf she could be with her words of unwisdom. "I'm sorry," she said again. "I just …"

"He didn't kill himself," he said, as if he understood her rambling.

Morgan let free a quiet breath of relief. "Is it rude of me to ask what *did* happen?"

"It was accident." He stared away, and his jaw sounded tighter when he added, "A motorbike accident."

"If it was an accident, why are you feeling so guilty?" What did he think he could have done?

"Because it was an accident that could have been avoided."

"Were you there?"

He shook his head, shifted on the bench.

"Then, what do you think you could have changed, exactly?"

"He was sick."

Morgan let that sink in. "He was sick … but didn't die of the sickness?"

"Nobody knew he was sick." His shoulders heaved alongside the sigh he released. "Except me."

"Was he getting treatment? Sorry—what was wrong with him?"

"He kept having blackouts. Just spacing out, like he couldn't hear, or see me. A couple of times, he even dropped. *Boosh.*" He sliced a hand through the air. "Just … straight down like I dunno what. And then he'd blink a minute later and carry on talking like he hadn't just checked out on me."

"And nobody else saw these … episodes?"

He shrugged. "He said not. Who knows? I just know he wouldn't let *me* tell anyone. And even though he kept promising me he'd go see the doc about it, I don't think he ever did."

"You think he was having one of these blackouts when he had the accident." She didn't ask it as a question.

He nodded. "He hit a road sign opposite a junction. Like he hadn't even tried turning for the bend." He turned toward her, the pain over rehashing the details an almost palpable force pumping from him. "He wouldn't have done that. I know he wouldn't."

"Were there any witnesses?"

He shook his head. "Unlike me, he *did* work farm hours. Not many others on the roads at that time in the morning."

"I'm sorry," she said, repeating her earlier condolence. She could say it a million times, though, and it would never be enough. She knew. She'd heard it over and over and over, herself. People liked to say the words to make you feel better, but they never did. Maybe they only existed to make the speaker feel more comfortable with the situation. No sense in everyone feeling crap, right?

"Thanks," he muttered, likely his reflex response, and suddenly Morgan didn't feel like she deserved his appreciation. Two little words could never lessen the blow of death. No amount of words could.

Before she could second-guess herself, she twisted fully around to face him, gripped hold of his broad shoulders and pulled him toward her until he gave in and rested his head alongside her own. She gently rubbed over his shoulder blades through his thick busman's coat. "It wasn't your fault," she told him.

Whoever Luke had been, he was an adult, responsible for himself. We could all advise each other in life, all give encouragement where we believed encouragement to be due, but not a single one of us had the right to force action on others. And the driver would realise, even accept, that with time.

When he didn't respond to her words, she added, "And your friend wouldn't want you believing it is, either."

After a few seconds filled with only breaths, he said, "I know."

He pulled back from her embrace. Slowly, almost as if he held reluctance over producing space between them. When she rubbed at his upper arm, he nodded like she'd asked him a question. "I should probably get to it." He pointed toward the front of the bus. "Next run is about to start."

She merely nodded in response. Watched as he silently packed up his rucksack, as he tucked away the cup she'd used, pulled the drawstring tight, clipped it closed. With a last glance toward her, one cowled by shadows and inadmissible of any discerning emotions, he lumbered his way down the length of the bus before enclosing himself in front of the wheel.

Ordinarily, Morgan would pack up herself. Grab any rubbish to take home and roll her way down to her usual seat. For some reason, she didn't feel inclined to move, but she couldn't seem to fight her routine and found herself back where she'd started the journey, sank into the bench she always took, leaning against the patch of wall against which she always leaned.

The next run through the towns garnered two or three more passengers than the previous one. Climbing on. Hopping off. All of them paying little mind to anything beyond themselves. The entire drive, she contemplated what she should do herself. Stay on? Get off? Although he hadn't rebuked her comforting, the driver hadn't exactly seemed ecstatic about it, either. Had she overstepped a boundary?

Maybe she should give him space.

When the stretch of road leading to her stop eventually showed up, Morgan pushed to her feet and wandered along the aisle to the bus platform. Holding onto the pole, she spied on the driver from the corner of her eye, caught the overt sideways glance from him, as if he needed to check who stood awaiting leave. Four times, her mouth opened to say something. To check he was okay. To let him know she'd had a nice journey—idiotic, considering how it had ended.

God, why couldn't she just make *normal* conversation, like *normal* people? Why did everything have to be strained and such hard work?

The bus gave a low squeal as it braked at the bus stop. The doors hissed their way open.

For a moment, she just stood there, staring, though what she looked for, she didn't know. Maybe she just hoped he'd ask her to stay. Tell her he'd really like it if they could talk a little more.

Instead, he said, "This is you, then."

"This is me," she said, trying to assess the low softness of his voice.

"Maybe I'll see you again."

That would be nice.

I hope so.

Would you like to grab a coffee sometime?

All words that would have been acceptable—even suitable—for the occasion, but being Morgan, she merely lifted a hand, gave a slight wave. "Bye."

And she hopped down from the bus into the freezing, slushy mound of snow that'd amassed in her absence.

Behind her, the doors clicked, signalling their closure, and she spun, almost skidding in her haste. "I'm Morgan!" she shouted at the last moment.

A muffled reply just squeezed through before the doors bumped together.

But as the bus pulled off, she realised she had no clue what it was.

CHAPTER 10

MARCEY'S ON ME. 2. LOOK LIVELY.

That had been the text that woke Morgan around four hours after she'd fallen asleep. A sleep borne of exhaustion, to which her rotating brain had contributed. How on earth Brandon could expect her to look anywhere near lively, after the past few days of wonky sleep she'd had, was beyond her. Still, she'd tried—if only to avoid the telling off she'd surely earn if she didn't. Bad enough getting one of those in the privacy of her own flat, let alone in public with an audience who'd probably stop everything they were doing just for the entertainment of it all. One time, when Bran had given his too-loud opinion, she'd even had to put up with that of some random woman who decided she wholeheartedly agreed with Brandon's assessment and then some. Apparently, Morgan was a 'pretty girl'—if she'd just apply a little makeup, dress a little smarter, then other people would be able to see that, too.

Morgan almost blushed in embarrassment all over again, just recalling the episode. Had she not still been climbing her way out of the grief hole, she might have told the woman to stick it. That the options of others accounted for little, in her books.

Dress for *yourself*. Achieve big for *yourself*. Look nice for *yourself*. Words her gran had thrown at her often as Morgan grew up. Especially when she'd started dating and would spend hours in her bedroom at Gran's house trying to decide what to wear and what to do with her hair, and would tell her grandmother 'I just want to look nice for him'. She could still remember how fast her gran's finger would start wagging at that.

Morgan had applied her gran's teachings to every date since her late teens. She just never applied them to Brandon because … well, he was Brandon, she guessed, and she knew him well enough to understand it wasn't *him* he wanted her to look nice for. He just wanted her to feel good, and to him, looking good was a part of that.

Bramwell Road hooked onto Little Spartan Street, and just after the bus Morgan had hopped onto made the turn, it pulled up at the stop in Freston town centre. With it being the end of the route, every passenger on board stood at the same time as Morgan, and every one of them also zombied their way into the aisle, somehow managing to slot between those who'd beat them to it without bouncing off one another. The way they all slipped into line, rolled their way forward, popped back out of line at the other end, onto the pavement, reminded Morgan of the conveyor belts at mass-production sites.

While some snow remained, a lot of it had turned to brown, slippery slush in the town. Thankfully, Morgan's 'best' boots had just enough grip to prevent her going arse over end, and she navigated her way through the stream of passengers, breaking free to the left at the first hint of a gap.

Lining the walls of the nearby department store building, bodies rested against brickwork in anticipation of their next bus, and head ducked into her shoulders against the chilly air, she passed them all toward the main stretch of shops and amenities.

Doors to an undercover mall jerked open and shut with the visitors passing through them. Morgan joined those pushing inside, into the warmth, easing her aggression once she'd succeeded on reaching the other side, where she took in the window displays of handmade chocolates and boutique clothing and sparkling rings as she walked.

Soft-toned Christmas tunes leaked from the overhead speakers. High ceilings held low lighting that set the tone of the venue, allowing a slight element of privacy to those using the open plan eatery, or those nipping into the underwear store for big-breasted women. Shoe stores. High street clothing. Sports brands. Coffee shops. So many units in one compact space.

Around two corners and up an escalator flight, Morgan found herself on the level containing the mass of eateries, and she headed toward Marcey's, two down on the right, gaze already trained on the window in search of her friend because she knew he'd already be there. He always was.

And just as she expected him to be, he already stared outward in search of her. He smiled the instant their eyes met, and the next second consisted of a quick up and down as he scanned her outfit.

"There," he said, as she slipped through the open doors and reached the table, "that wasn't so hard to look like an actual human being now, was it?"

"Shut up," she said, leaning in to kiss the cheek he angled toward her.

"I already grabbed you a Frappuccino." He pushed one

of two paper cups he guarded toward the seat opposite him. "Didn't know what you fancied to eat, though, so I waited."

"Good of you," she said, slipping into the awaiting hard, plastic chair. After shrugging her coat from her shoulders, she reached for the menu, read through the small selection on offer. Sandwiches—not regular sandwiches, but ones filled with Alaskan line-caught fish, or thickly-sliced Wiltshire ham from free-range piggies. Baked potatoes, made from organically produced spuds and filled to bursting with locally sourced amazingness. Salad descriptions that read like purple prose. And crisps—even those hand-baked and crunchy enough to pierce gums. Morgan could just imagine some woman on the telly announcing everything in a low, seductive voice, trying to convince anyone listening that they just *had* to taste everything on offer, if only in an effort to come across as sexy as she. As good as it all sounded, though, a quick glance around at the other diners' plates showed just regular-looking sarnies and slightly over-baked spuds. "I'll just have a sandwich, I think."

Brandon pushed up to his feet, but paused before turning away completely. "I'll get you a salad to go with that." His finger swirled in the air. "You eat too many cakes to not have salad, once in a while."

"Oh, stop it," she said, but he'd already marched away.

In typical Brandon style, he once again sported trousers that barely reached his ankles. The jacket he'd donned over the white T-shirt she'd spotted had its sleeves rolled most of the way up his forearms. And he wore ridiculous footwear for a cold winter day, once again over sockless feet. Some days, Morgan wondered if he even had any feeling in them, how they didn't turn blue—his whole body, even. Or maybe he was just some kind of alien, or anomaly, that she shouldn't try figuring out.

Heck, who was she kidding. She'd quit trying to work Brandon out a long time ago. Brandon just *was*. And Morgan kinda loved him for it.

After almost five minutes of leaning slightly over the tinsel-adorned counter, his arse kicked out in a pose she recognised as Brandon's flirting stance, he spun away with a tray in hand, hips jiggling so hard the contents swished from side-side across the laminated veneer. It was a wonder the diners either side of him didn't end up wearing their food. She half expected them all to duck away as he passed through.

"Ham, pickle and cheese," he said, swinging a plate down with flourish.

Beneath her nose sat a doorstep-thick sandwich, but at least the bread looked lovely and fresh.

"Ready salted." The packet of crisps landed with a slap beside her plate. "And because I know how much you love them, I got the salad to share." Popping down the greens, and a plated sandwich for himself, he slid back into his seat and vanished the tray into the runners beneath the table. "And don't think I've forgotten why we're here," he said, biting a chunk from his lunch.

Of course he hadn't forgotten. Brandon rarely forgot a thing—especially when it pertained to gossip he wanted in on.

That didn't mean Morgan wouldn't make him work for it, though. Feigning innocence—or maybe ignorance—she lifted her sandwich and studied it like it really did look as delicious as its menu description. "So, what have you been up to?" she asked, before taking a bite and filling her mouth with enough food to prevent normal conversation.

He stared hard at her, like he knew exactly what her game was. "Since yesterday?"

She nodded, managed a, "Hm-mm."

"Sleeping at *normal* hours, like a *normal* person. And working. As you well know." He snapped out a lettuce leaf and, after crunching off a bite, jabbed it toward her. "What about you? What have *you* been up to, sweets?" Asked in a tone of voice that suggested he already knew the answer. Even if he did, that wouldn't be enough for him. He'd want it verbalised. Excavated. Turned inside out to lay bare its innards and exposed for his scrutiny.

Really wishing her cheeks didn't heat so darned easily, she placed her sandwich back down. "I caught the bus again."

A small smile slid across his lips.

"Just like you told me to."

"And?"

She let out a long sigh, fingers fiddling with the corner of her sandwich, almost triumphant when Brandon's shoulders sagged and his smile slipped.

"He wasn't there." He didn't ask it as a question, more a cocktail of resignation and disappointment, and as much as she wanted to drag out the pretence and torture him more, she seemed to have little control over the bushfire happening beneath her flesh and the way her lips fought against her to twist into a weird, lopsided grin. "Morgan King, you are glowing like a bloody beacon." He reached over and pressed his fingers to her face before snapping them back with a, "*Tsssss.* You are red hot. *Spill!*"

A small giggle escaped before she could stop it.

"Oh, Lord," Brandon said, lifting his gaze toward the ceiling, "please forgive the violence with which I am about to shake my best friend if she doesn't tell me, im-*me*-diately, why she's acting like a crushing teenager."

She reached across and shoved him. "Stop it." Least of

all because the closest diners suddenly paid less attention to their meals and more attention to what was happening at Morgan's table. "Or I'm telling my gran you're using her beloved Lord in vain." A decent threat. Her gran visited church every Sunday, whatever the weather, and considered it her only failing as a grandparent that Morgan didn't join her as often as she'd have liked.

His head flopped back down. "Please don't tell her. She already thinks I'm trouble."

"She does *not* think you're trouble," Morgan said, laughing. "She adores you."

"Yes, well." He brushed at his shoulders. "Many people do, honey. But I digress ..."

"Okay, okay." She held up her hands, amusement still tugging at her lips. "Begin the interrogation. Might as well get it over with."

"You make me sound like the bloody gestapo." He sniffed.

"No comment."

"How does the saying go? If you're going to brand me a liar, I might as well be one?" The smile he gave held elements of knowing sass with a touch of evil. "What happened when you caught the bus, sweet cheeks? Was the mystery *drüüver* on board?"

"Maybe," she hedged, resting her chin atop her curled fingers.

"Don't you play coy with me, lady."

She sighed. "Okay, yes. Happy?"

"Not even." He leaned in close and stared hard. Unblinking and focused as heck.

Morgan knew, from experience, that Brandon could keep it up for far longer than herself. She'd seen him go until tears streamed his cheeks and the whites of his eyes turned red. She didn't particularly want to witness that again. "Fine, you win."

With a satisfied smirk, he relaxed in his seat and snapped up a piece of lettuce he deposited in his mouth with a crunch.

"The new driver *was* on the bus again—you don't think something has happened to George, do you? I hate to think—"

"You're deflecting," Brandon said, still chewing through bits of salad.

She was—though only to a degree, because she *was* worried about George.

"So, what happened? Did you talk again?"

"We did."

"Please tell me it was more interesting than your last awful conversation."

"It was. Kind of."

Brandon's eyebrow arched up.

"And then it sort of …"

"Sort of *what?*"

"It sort of … all went a bit wrong."

Brandon raised his hands skyward. "Oh, Lord, saveth me from this hopeless specimen before me."

"Don't be so dramatic." Trying to ignore the way more diners had started to glance over, she reached across and tugged his arms down. "Stop it, you idiot."

"Seriously, sugar, you have something wrong with you, I swear."

"Everybody has something wrong with them."

He rolled his eyes. "Whatever. How did it go downhill, sweets? What'd you do?"

"Oh, so it's *my* fault?"

"Why, was it his?"

"Maybe it was nobody's."

"And we're back to deflecting. Are you going to tell me what happened, or am I going to have to stand on my chair and start quoting Shakespeare tragedies?"

"You do that, and I'll never lunch with you again."

"If you don't start talking, I'll never lunch *with you* again." He smiled like he'd just one-upped her. And maybe he had, because Brandon had many other friends he could be spending his time with. Morgan had ... well, she pretty much just had her gran.

"Fine," she muttered. "Just ... promise me you'll quit with the theatrics."

CHAPTER 11

EVERYTHING HAPPENS IN THREES.

Brandon's words bounced around inside Morgan's head, as she stepped from the bus two streets over from Chumbrey. Of course, she could have stayed on for another few minutes, gotten closer to home, but closer to home meant farther from High Street, and if she was going to let her annoying friend prod her into a nighttime outing for the third, very early morning in a row, she'd be needing supplies of the baked variety.

Sprinkles Of Joy nearly always had a queue, even if only a small one. Partly because, Morgan suspected, it was close to bus stops, and possibly because a good reputation can spread from shoppers just as easily as a bad one. Thankfully, she rounded the doorway to find only three other patrons stood before her, and she spent the time waiting behind them scanning over the glass displays and the tempting goods they protected.

"You decided?" Lou asked when the path before her had cleared out. Lou had worked at Sprinkles for as long as Morgan could remember visiting there. With brown, coarse hair tucked backward beneath a netted hat, and boobs big enough to push the boundaries of the bottle green apron she wore over her regular clothes, she stood with hands turned outward, knuckles on hips, smiling down at Morgan from her five-ten height. Oddly, despite her stature and oh, so tempting place of work, Lou never seemed to carry even an ounce of excess fat anywhere on her body, apart from her chest.

"I think I might keep it simple today," Morgan said. "Especially as those doughnuts look extra powdered and extra filled."

"I must have known you'd be in," Lou said with a wink. "Two, is it?"

"Yes, please."

Lou bustled to it, and a minute, or so later, Morgan found herself back outside in the cold, her hands gently cupping a bag of doughnuts that still felt warm. Her breath lightly fogged the cold air almost immediately, and rather than dally until the chill of it could seep into her bones, she set off on the walk home. As she went, she couldn't help but explore the differences between her hometown and where the bus driver lived. Her feet trod tarmaced pavement. Her periphery caught on uniformed houses, followed by uniformed bungalows, each lit by sparkling lights the dulling daylight didn't fully display, cars zooming by in sloshy whizzes on her other side. Scattered between those, skinny columns of grey, topped by the street's lighting she couldn't be bothered to glance up toward.

He probably walked along ungenerous grass verges to get anywhere, drove along one-track lanes to go farther, waved over hedgerows to neighbours and farmers, and laughed heartily with everyone in the local pub, all of them merry and filled with the fresh air and relaxation of the surrounding countryside.

Morgan sighed as she tried to imagine living in such a place. Would she miss the hustle and bustle? The noise? The busyness of everyone?

If asked when in a strong relationship, she'd have said no. That living in a small and close community in the centre of nature sounded like bliss.

As a single woman, though? No one to share her home with? No one with whom to share her highs and lows? It sounded isolating and lonely.

Besides, she thought, the rustle of paper between her hands reminding her of the doughnuts, just think of the baked goods she'd be missing out on.

A light buzzing hit her body, the tinny tinkle of her mobile breaking in before she could counter argue over the stereotype of country women with aprons and mixing bowls, and she drew it free to check the screen. The corners of her mouth twitched outward as soon as she saw the caller's name, and she hit to answer as she lifted it to her ear.

"Hi, Gran."

"Who is this?" came the aged voice down the line. "Why are you calling me? I don't understand. I'm so confused."

"Very funny, Gran."

A sigh hit Morgan's ear. "Try telling those parents of yours."

"They worry about you." Or they'd used to, anyway. Once upon a time. Didn't stop Morgan trying to convince her gran, though, even if she didn't feel particularly convinced of her words herself.

"I haven't heard from them in over three months."

Neither had Morgan, come to think of it. Her fly-away and fancy-free parents had both 'retired' young. Enriched with an artistic talent he'd passed on to Morgan, her father had announced he needed new and warmer pastures in which to continue his passion. Obviously, her mother had gone along with it, but it hadn't been that much of a contest. She could have put her foot down and continued working in the local doctors' surgery, if she'd really wanted —instead, she'd put in for her pension packet and flitted off to Javea, where she'd since roamed shops, drank wine, and frolicked with the local women she'd befriended, whilst Morgan's dad splashed paint onto canvases he sold mostly to tourists.

That move had been made almost five years before, and Morgan and her gran seemed to hear from them less and less. As if the sun and alcohol got to them a little more with each sip and wiped the family they'd left behind from their memories a tiny bit more with each passing year.

"I'm sure they'll call next week," Morgan said, praying they would. If they didn't, she'd be kicking up a storm herself.

"Oh, yes, speaking of next week. I wanted to check if you're still coming."

Morgan frowned—not because she didn't understand the non-question, but because she couldn't quite believe it had been asked.

"For Christmas dinner," Gran added, like she wouldn't know. "You *are* still coming, aren't you?"

"Am I allowed to call *you* ridiculous right now?"

"Well, you never know …"

"Gran, you're being ridiculous. There, I said it." She kicked her feet back into action, rounding a woman sliding a pushchair over the slippery ground. "I'm offended you felt the need to ask me that."

"Can you cover dessert?" she continued, obviously choosing to ignore Morgan's line of conversation.

"Yes, Gran." Morgan always covered dessert. Just like she'd always gone to her gran's for Christmas dinner. Every. single. year. since her parents had moved away and Morgan had gotten a place of her own. And for quite a few years prior to that, too. "I've already ordered it."

"From Sprinkles?"

"Yes, ma'am."

"You're such a good girl."

"Because I bring you good cake?"

"Well, why else?" Gran's laughter tinkled like bells down the line, and Morgan couldn't help but smile. "So, is there anything else?" she added, like Morgan was pestering her.

"You called me, remember?"

"Then, I'll see you next week. Don't be late."

"I won't, Gran."

"Dinner will spoil, if you're late."

"I don't see how I can possibly be late, Gran, when I'll be there the night before."

"I love you, dear," came down the line, and then her gran hung up.

Shaking her head, Morgan slipped her phone away, and as she continued on toward home, she told herself the smile that clung to her lips had everything to do with the nutso phone call she'd just had.

And absolutely nothing to do with the trip she'd most likely be taking that night.

CHAPTER 12

ANOTHER DAY. ANOTHER RIDICULOUS HOUR.

Part of Morgan wondered if, without the clock set, she'd sleep right on past when she usually woke. Like, maybe it wouldn't happen for the second night in a row when she actually wanted it to. And that, maybe, it would be a sign that she shouldn't be piddling about catching buses while most *normal* folks were sleeping and she should tell the insects in her stomach over a guy she barely knew to buzz off.

But no. A little after one in the morning, she stood sipping steamy liquid from an oversized mug and wondering whether *she* was the only ridiculous thing in her life right then.

As she could have predicted, she spent the first thirty minutes of being awake wandering the flat and resisting the urge to catch that bloody bus. And also as she could have predicted, she found herself standing in the spare bedroom, staring at the painting Brandon had so scrutinised a couple of days earlier. From the earthy blends of colour, rough lines, scratched in criss-crosses and swishes of paint, to the slightly darker outline of what could actually be … a jaw?

Swallowing, Morgan allowed her gaze to drift upward, over where a nose ought to be—if she had in any way created a face—and a little higher, to where dark eyes would be gazing out with warmth and little bit of humour and just enough *something* to make her stomach pitter-patter …

Just as the dark shapes peering back at her from the painting did right then.

But they weren't eyes. No way were they eyes. Because then she'd have to admit there might be some kind of features beginning to form in her painting, and she didn't want to. She certainly didn't want to admit that, oh hell, Brandon could be right. Not when 'right' was his favourite place to be and she'd never hear the end of it.

"Ridiculous," she muttered to herself. Another ridiculous thing to add to her life.

With a huff and a swing of her mug, she spun away from the easel and stomped from the room.

GOD, she was so *obvious*.

So obvious in pretending she wouldn't be going anywhere.

So obviously going to give in and admit she *would be* going somewhere.

So obviously going to end up pulling on warm clothes and trudging outside into weather the forecaster had fore-warned wouldn't really improve, even as the snow started to melt.

Which was why Morgan found herself, once again, freezing and shivering in frigid air in which most sensible people avoided finding themselves. Although the central section of the pavements had been trodden down and sullied, the outer edges had formed into small mounds of whiteness, only the occasional blip to their perfection created by people having stepped closer to the kerb. In both directions, tiny diamond-like sparkles bordered the road, as Morgan stood stomping her booted feet, surrounded by a mist of her own departed breath.

Thank goodness she'd remembered her gloves.

She half expected the bus to be late again thanks to the continued weather, but almost smack on time, she caught the tiny growl of its engine, chased by the appearance of headlights up at the corner.

As it slowed near the stop, small sprays of melting slush arced up onto the kerbs. Morgan took a small step back, putting the tiny tingles running beneath her skin down to the cold, and waited until the bus had stopped completely before moving forward again. With their usual hiss, the doors flapped open, and she climbed up into the warmth of her haven, barely able to control the grin trying to take over her face.

"'Morning," she called, bakery bag held at chest height, lest he miss her intention.

"How 'you doin', kid?"

Going from the darkness of outside, it took a fraction of a second for her eyes to adjust and confirm who the voice belonged to.

"Oh … George. Hi."

"Who were you expecting? George Clooney?"

"George Clooney is a little old for me, don't you think?"

"You young uns." He jerked his chin over his shoulder. "Go on and sit down now. You're letting in all the cold."

With a nod, Morgan drifted off down the aisle, her chest

filled with a deflation she had no idea how to interpret. She didn't get disappointed about seeing George. George was her reason for catching the bus in the middle of the night. Had been for the past couple of years.

So, why was she suddenly wishing he was somebody else?

A certain someone else with a small flop of brown hair and a smile that changed his entire face when he showed it.

Barely even seeing the other passengers, Morgan moved toward her regular seat, even twisted to wiggle in, but halted when her eyes connected with those of a tired-looking guy and an expression that said he'd rather she stopped right there and turned herself around.

It had finally happened.

First, she'd caught the bus and George hadn't been driving.

And now somebody has stolen my seat.

How many changes could the world expect her to adapt to within the same week?

"Sorry," she muttered, turning away. On seeing the opposite seat free, she paused. She could, she supposed, have asked the intruder to take that seat instead. Explained to him that she usually sat where he'd chosen and how much she liked her routines and didn't really like having to change the details of her life without a little forethought.

Without obsessing, more like, her gran would say.

Yes, the rational part of her brain knew he wouldn't understand the workings of her mind—not when she didn't 'get' them herself. That, or he wouldn't care. So, taking a deep breath, she sank into the seat that *was* free, and settled herself in for the ride.

THE HAT MORGAN wore protected her temple from the cold window, against which she rested her head. Half-heartedly watching the streets pass by, between glancing up at new arrivals and those getting off, she solemnly counted down the stops between the bus and the city centre.

Would she stay on, as usual? Chat to George, as she always did?

Or had, until the previous night, anyway.

Or maybe she needed to leave the bus and try a new experience before getting the bus home. After all, occurrences were said to come in threes, and that would complete the trilogy of routine deviances for her, right?

In its usual fashion, the bus slowed nearer the end of its route. Also as usual, everyone but her started fidgeting, some already climbing from their seats to make their way toward the exit.

Morgan had always liked 'usual'. *Normal.* Patterns and order. They counteracted the disorder she often displayed in her art. Calmed the too-present chaos of her mind.

The two previous nights had been the first blip in that order, and if anyone had asked her prior to it happening, she'd have told them she'd hate it—that people had routines for a reason and they needed to be respected.

Except, she hadn't hated the small slips of time she'd gotten to spend with a perfect stranger. Not a single bit.

The bus finally stopped, the doors swinging aside and creating an opening over the same piece of pavement they always did, and Morgan stared down toward where the handful of passengers climbed from the bus and slunk off into the shadows of the city. She was still staring that way when the doors secured her inside, and George emerged from his space, and the low light at the front of the bus was all that remained to show the way.

George ambled his almost sixty-year-old body along the aisle, flask in hand, coming to a stop beside the bench where Morgan sat. "Why so blue tonight, kid?"

"Not blue," she said, moving only her eyes to look at him. "Just ..." She shrugged.

"You better come tell me all about it," he said, and he carried on along to the back of the bus, leaving Morgan to follow behind.

With a grunt and a heavy sigh, George climbed up onto the rear bench and patted the seat beside him, as he always did.

Accepting the invitation, Morgan settled herself where he'd indicated and held up her paper bag. "Custard doughnut do you?"

"It'll more than do."

"What's on your menu?" she asked, as he set his flask down on the facing seat.

"Hot chocolate. Anything else just wouldn't have worked against all this snow."

Morgan smiled. George always said odd little things like that. Maybe that was why she enjoyed his company. It meant she didn't have to be slightly odd all on her own.

"What happened to your jeans?" he asked, tapping just the tip of a finger against a blob of cerulean blue paint.

"Art happened."

"Ah." Twisting toward her, he studied her for a moment, before lightly tapping that same fingertip against the rim of her hat. "And what happened to your head?"

"I got the bus the last two nights," she said.

He lifted his chin in acknowledgment of her words, offered another, "Ah." Reaching over to the opposite seat, he unscrewed the mugs from the flask, carefully placing them down on the fabric, before equally as carefully pouring a portion of steaming hot chocolate into each. "I know you might find it hard to believe," he said, handing her one of the mugs, "but I do occasionally need time off, you know."

She sighed. "I know."

He lifted his mug. Took a sip. Said, "Did he kick you off? The other driver?"

"No, thankfully." Her lips curved at the memory. "He was going to, but ..."

"You talked him 'round. Aye," he said, nodding. "You're good at that."

"It didn't take much effort, to be fair."

"*I* didn't take much effort."

"You didn't take any effort, at all."

He raised his mug as if in toast. "Like I said."

Morgan released a quiet laugh.

"So, what has that pretty face of yours looking all dour, then?"

"Oh, nothing really."

"It ain't nothing when you come onto my bus all frowning on seeing me."

"I didn't frown." She frowned then. "Did I?"

With a wry smile, he gave a nod of his head.

"Sorry. It's just .... God, I don't even know."

"Was he mean to you—this chap from last night?"

"No, he was nice."

"He was, eh?"

"Yes, he sat at the back with me when I asked him to."

"That so?" he said, taking his plastic mug toward his lips.

"Although, he did insist on sitting way at the other side of the bench."

"Yeah, well ... you can be quite terrifying."

"Hey!" She lightly elbowed his side, before sighing and thinking back to the nights before.

"Talk to me." George gently nudged her with his own elbow. "And get the doughnuts out, if you ever planned to share."

The bag rustled as she offered it to George first, but she didn't reach in for her own. "The driver last night was nice," she said.

"We covered that one," George said around his mouthful.

"I don't know what else to say." Not to George, anyway. Not when she didn't even know what to *think*.

"I take it he talked to you?"

"He did, yes. Reluctantly at first, but … he seemed to … just give in, I guess."

"Or maybe he quit trying to figure you out and just went with it."

"Maybe."

He took another bite of his sugary ball, chewing before asking, "So, what did the two of you talk about?"

Morgan shrugged. "Mostly just about why I was catching buses in the middle of the night when I don't actually go anywhere other than back home again." She could have went on to tell him how the driver had also shared a little piece of himself, about his sadness and how she'd spent the past twenty-four hours wishing she knew how to take that sadness away and make it her own. What was a bit more to add to that she already carried?

Except, it was far from her story to tell.

"Did he run away at that point?" George asked, the hint of laughter in his tone bringing her back round.

"No, actually."

"I'm impressed."

"Hey!" she said for a second time, needling his ribs again.

"I meant with *you*."

Her half-smile faded. "Why me?"

"Okay, maybe him, too."

She wobbled her head, eyebrows raised in question.

"Well, you must've told him all about yourself within, what? Five, ten minutes of talking?"

"I told *you* all about myself when we just met."

"Actually, it took until about your fourth journey with me before you finally opened up and talked."

"No, I—" she started, but stopped at his nodding. "Surely not."

"Surely so."

"Wow," she muttered. That was *not* how she remembered it. At all.

"Must've been a pretty special driver manning my bus the last couple of nights."

"Maybe." Another mutter.

"That, or you're not quite as lost as you once were." He nudged her with his knee as he climbed to his feet. "Come on now, back to your seat." Scooping up his flask, he brushed past her and stepped down into the aisle. "You can give your cup back when you leave. And *eat* something," he added as he walked away.

Morgan watched George all the way to the front of the bus, where he ducked back into his driving kiosk and knocked the lights back on. Then she hauled herself up and back to where she'd been sitting earlier. For a moment, she considered climbing up into the seat she'd occupied every other time she'd caught the bus, but she'd already survived having to move once, hadn't she? Something had forced her out of a habit and she hadn't freaked out, or had a meltdown, and didn't feel full of distress at the idea of sitting somewhere else.

Not anymore, anyway.

Ignoring the pull toward the bench on her right, she edged into the one on the left, settling herself in with her hot chocolate with one hand, while reaching in for her doughnut with the other.

A moment later, the bus rumbled to life, gave a slight wobble, then started off on its loop around the island to the first stop of the journey across the street.

As two passengers climbed aboard, Morgan allowed them each a cursory glance before tucking into her meal. Neither of them looked her way. That was the trouble with commuting. Some might call it social travel, which was pretty ironic really, considering so few who used it wanted to make eye contact, let alone fully engage. A lonely existence while surrounded by others.

It was a lifestyle Morgan had come to know well. A lifestyle she might have, at one time, embraced. A lot had changed in her over the past year, though. And even more had changed in the space of two nights.

One by one, passengers boarded along the route before hopping off later down the line, and before Morgan knew it, George pulled up at the stop nearest her apartment.

His door clicked open, and he poked his head out. "You going, or staying a while?"

She thought about it for a moment before shifting from her seat. "Going."

Ignoring the curious stares of the passengers, because anything different to their considered norm could get them looking, apparently, she edged her way to the front, where she handed over her empty mug. "Thanks for the hot chocolate."

"Thanks for the doughnut," he said, taking the cup.

"And thanks for listening. As always."

"The guy who covered me last night?" At George's serious tone, she lifted her eyes to his. "His name is Tom Michaels."

So *that* was what he went by. Had that been what he'd shouted before those doors had stolen his voice? "Tom Michaels," she repeated, the name sounding almost angelic as it floated past her lips.

"He usually drives the eighty-seven bus."

With her heart suddenly beating a little harder, Morgan stared at him, unsure why he'd told her, yet totally aware all at the same time.

"Mornings 'til early afternoon are his regular hours." He smiled and winked. "Now, go get some sleep. Freshen up. You're going to need it."

"Thanks, George," she said, and hopped down from the bus with a smile on her face, onto a wintry street that no longer felt quite so cold.

CHAPTER 13

MORGAN HADN'T JUMPED OUT OF BED THE NEXT MORNING and raced to the eighty-seven stop. As much as she'd wanted to, the same brain sending encouragement also paralysed her with nerves and worry, and a full day had passed before she managed to ignore her inner stress and kick her own arse out into the melting snow and lingering cold.

In the grey, wintry daylight, her breaths misted the air before her, the moment she stepped outside and began her careful walk along the pavement. A few gardens down from her own, a neighbour whose name she'd never learned uprighted a wooden cutout of a reindeer.

She glanced up, gave a small wave and a roll of her eyes. "Bloody kids," she said, half-pointing to the offended reindeer.

"You'd think the snow would give them enough to do," Morgan said as she continued on past.

"You'd think," the woman called after her.

Less blinding during the day, yet in far more abundance, lights blinked at Morgan from every direction. Out of windows, from between tree branches, unabashedly from the fronts of properties and out of the beard of one man she passed. Lights everywhere on that dull, dull day, as if in an effort to remind all of the brightness of the month. The excitement and anticipation of what was to come.

For many, anyway.

Morgan tried not to dwell too hard on those left alone at a time when most came together. Especially as, if not for her gran, she'd probably be among them herself.

When she finally reached Chumbrey High Street, the queue at Sprinkles Of Joy reached the door, which was a fairly conservative length, considering lunchtime loomed near and more people than usual often flocked to the bakery for their outstanding seasonal range of baked goods. Standing just beyond the tinseled doorway, eyes squinting past the sporadic fairy lights lining the windows, Morgan took the time to carefully consider the menu, trying to focus past the tap-tap-tapping of feet by the man in front of her. She didn't usually need to concentrate so hard, because she *usually* just ordered whatever looked the most tempting from the display, but she needed to be sure for once. Needed just the right choice to accompany the boldness she hadn't cared to display for too long. Sure, because if everything went pear-shaped, at least one of the choices she made that day needed to be a good one.

From a speaker somewhere inside, the radio played *All I Want For Christmas Is You* beneath the humdrum of customers ordering and thanking and leaving the store, each time creating less of a gap between Morgan and the counter.

"What'll it be?" the bakery owner asked when Morgan finally reached her. "Cinnamon roll? Cookie? Or something savoury, for a change?"

Morgan smiled at Lou behind the counter, knowing

she'd likely surprise her with her latest selection, she said, "Two fresh cream, red velvet cupcakes please."

Lou's eyebrow lifted.

"In a box."

"Well, well, well," she said, already unfolding the cake box and shaking her head. "I hope these aren't both for you. They're much more filling than your usual."

"They aren't," Morgan admitted.

"Thatta girl." With a wink, she popped two of the indulgent cakes into the box and handed them over. "You'll have to tell me how you get on."

"I will. And keep the change," she said, leaving a fiver on the counter.

From the bakery, she navigated away from home for a short way, taking a turn onto Merryway Road and heading for a stop she'd never had much use for before, not with its far more direct route to the city centre's edge before continuing on to the next county over.

A small queue had formed at the stop. Probably because the bus was near due—information Morgan had looked into prior to leaving the apartment. Joining the back of it, she found herself humming along to *Anti-Lullaby* by Karen-O, a song she found soothing, despite the underlying darkness to it.

As one minute passed, followed by two, she dipped into the dangerous territory of questioning her plan. What if she got on the bus and he wasn't even driving?

What if he was driving but had no idea who she was?

She glanced over her shoulder, considered making a hasty getaway before she'd be confronted with a definite decision, but more people had joined the queue, boxing her in from behind. She'd have to weave her way around everyone else just to leave.

"Henry, come on now. The bus is coming."

Morgan spun back around to see a young boy sliding in close to what must have been his mother and taking her hand. And beyond them, the front of the bus loomed large and intimidating as it squealed to a halt at the bus stop's exit.

Bodies around her hustled in tighter, all of them made larger by their winter coats and warm clothing, giving her little choice but to be carried forward on their wave of movement. Before she even had a chance to fully panic, she'd reached the entryway to the bus's steps, and with a passenger to her side, another at her back, she stepped up onto the platform and raised her face, the hugged bakery box already at chest height in offering.

Hair shorned close to the scalp topped the driver's head. And when grey eyes met hers, she stopped so abruptly, she almost tumbled into the dividing perspex, the passenger behind her bumping her back.

"You—you don't look like how I expected," she stuttered. "How I remember."

He half-smiled, half-frowned. "How did you expect me to look?"

When she glanced down to his name badge, her lips popped open. *Mark Romaine.* "You're not Tom," she said, meeting his eyes again.

"Which Tom is that, then?"

Ignoring the tutting and slight shoves from behind, she said, "Tom Michaels?"

"Ah, that Tom. I know him."

"Is he working today?" She could always fight her way off and wait for a different eighty-seven, after all.

"Nah, it's his day off. Did a couple of nights for a change, didn't he? Means he gets a few days to rest now."

"Oh ... right," she said, already trying to back herself away into the huffing mob of awaiting passengers.

"I can give him a message," the driver said, and she paused in her escape.

"You can?"

"You want, I can tell him you were looking for him."

Did she want that? Wouldn't it make her seem a bit forward?

Or needy, even?

Was that really the kind of impression she wanted to give?

"Oh, erm, no, it's okay," she said, feeling the bump of another passenger already trying to push around her to the front. "I mean, I only met him on the night bus, and ..." Fire flamed through her cheeks as soon as she realised how ridiculous she sounded. "Never mind."

With best elbow forward, she nudged her way off the bus, ignoring the *"Finally!"* she caught from one of the passengers as she hopped down to the pavement and took off at a march.

Stupid. Stupid Morgan.

Her cheeks still held enough heat to ward off the cold, and her pounding chest took care of the rest of her body. Down the street she marched, face lowered so she didn't have to see the irritation and nosiness of those still nudging forward in the queue. Only once she'd passed them all by a good twenty paces did she lift her face enough to take in the street.

In the shady doorway of a closed barbershop, a bundle of blankets surrounded a pair of world-weary eyes. Morgan veered off that way, her chest tight with enough emotion and embarrassment to crush it, and closer, she stooped down and held out the box that'd become crumpled at the corners. After all, what could she possibly want with the cakes anymore?

"Merry Christmas," she said, even though there were a good few days yet to pass.

The hand that emerged from the tatty fabrics shook slightly and carried little meat and muscle, and Morgan reached closer to preserve the person's energy.

"Just a couple of cakes, but you might enjoy them," she said.

She received a small nod of acknowledgement, a blink of eyes that filled with suspicion, as if the bearer had no experience in kindness, as if they'd lived only a life of cruelty and disappointment. And didn't that just add to the sadness in her heart.

"You could use a hat, too," she said, taking in the hair that protruded in many directions from beneath the thread-bare wool. She tugged the one from her head, trying not to stare too longingly down at it. "This one is fleece-lined, keeps out the cold winds and works a treat to keep your ears warm?"

A second hand stretched out, and a slight shrug knocked the blanket from his head, revealing unkempt and obviously unwashed hair that looked darker than the blond she guessed it might've been. The hat vanished from her hands and got slid over those dirty locks all the way down to the man's eyebrows. That time, when he nodded, a slight hint of gratitude and respect glinted in his eyes, before he rustled through the bag and pulled out one of the cupcakes. "Merry Christmas to you, too," he bounced back in a voice all gravelly and hoarse like it'd gone underused.

With a nod of her own, Morgan straightened from her squat and went on her not so merry way, while trying to focus less on how cold her head suddenly felt and more on the deed she'd just done, ignoring that she didn't feel quite as elated as she maybe should have at doing something good. She didn't want to investigate the real reason for the lack of good mood. The failed attempt at taking matters into her own hands—taking her life into her own hands. She certainly didn't want to mull over just how ever-so-slightly devastated she'd felt upon seeing someone other than who she'd been looking for behind that damned bus wheel.

A few corners turned and streets walked, of trying not to think and blanking her mind, set Morgan back on the right navigational track.

Back toward her flat.

Back toward her empty life.

CHAPTER 14

POUNDING HIT THE FRONT DOOR OF MORGAN'S FLAT LIKE someone was trying to break through. Probably Brandon, she guessed. He'd called her the day after her bus journey with George. He'd called her the day after that and let her know just how appalled he was to find she was at home, in the flat, instead of on the eighty-seven bus already and hunting down Mr Floppy Hair, as he'd dubbed him. And when he'd called the day after that, she hadn't picked up, eventually placing her phone on silent to save her from his incessant attempts to get through and, no doubt, berate her. She'd felt deflated enough on finding the balls to get on the bloody bus, only to be faced with the wrong guy as it was, and with Christmas suddenly looming right over her head, finding it in herself to try again would just have to wait until she'd gotten the damned day over and done with.

If not for her gran, she might not have bothered celebrating the season, at all.

Another round of booming echoed through to where she stood in the spare bedroom, and sighing, Morgan placed her brush down on a paint-crusted cloth and swept her way through the flat. She pulled open the door just as a brown-uniformed guy was about to disappear.

"Hello?" she called after him in time for him to pause and turn back. "Sorry it took so long." *I thought you were my annoying friend.*

Her annoying friend who cared about her more than any other friend ever had and who'd go to the ends of the earth and back to help make her happy. Or to Australia, at least. Somewhere warm and sunny where he could top up his tan and his sockless ankles wouldn't get cold …

"Parcel for King." He held out a box made of thick, brown cardboard, and as soon as Morgan relieved him of it, stooping slightly beneath its weight, he pulled some device from his pocket and snapped a photo of her. "Proof of delivery," he said, waving his chunky camera-thing.

"Thanks," Morgan muttered, but he'd already whirled away and was vanishing once again.

Turning sideways, she manoeuvred herself inside the flat and shut the door. She wouldn' need to check the parcel papers to see who'd sent it. The airmail stickers offered information enough.

Every year, sometimes as early as November, sometimes barely scraping through in time, and sometimes mid-January or later, the same nondescript box arrived in the post, containing pretty much exactly the same items as the one that came before it. Her parents' version of *Merry Christmas,* and *See, we haven't forgotten you.* Personally, she kind of loved the parcels, but her gran? Morgan knew she'd prefer to just see them in person—that kind of gift would be worth a billion boxes through the post.

She dropped the box down in the middle of the living room before heading through and grabbing a sharp knife from the kitchen drawer. It took less than thirty seconds to slice through the multi layers of tape covering the box's seam, and Morgan smiled when she folded the flaps back out of the way and unwrapped the black tissue paper packing everything in tight.

Right at the very top of the contents sat three pairs of thick, soft, fluffy socks—where they'd found them in Spain, when her parents only ever bragged about the heat and the sunshine, she didn't know—and a couple of sets of what might have been hand-knitted mittens.

Straight away, Morgan tugged off the socks she'd been wearing and replaced them with one of the new pairs, before returning her attention to what sat beneath all the knitted goods. Food. Or more accurately: treats.

Of the best kind.

One by one, she drew each item out and lined them up on the coffee table ready for transferring into her kitchen cupboards.

Churros. Goodness, she *loved* traditional churros.

Turron, which always set her teeth on edge but she couldn't seem to stop eating once she started.

Ponche Caballen. Morgan never quite knew if she was supposed to use it in cooking, or drink it, but always seemed to end up going with the latter. Especially if Brandon found the bottle when visiting.

Pastelles de yema. Three packets. Morgan might have mentioned to her parents' *multiple times* how much those were her favourites.

Palmeritas came out next. Followed by aged olive oils and vinegars. Brandon always accused her of not eating enough salad, but the truth was, a salad without a dressing made from beautifully sourced ingredients just didn't satisfy. And last, but not least, a tin of Bizcochos Noel de Lerma— her parents' version of a Christmas card.

For a few moments, Morgan sat surrounded by her spoils, feeling somewhat satisfied by their presence, and even slightly appeased with her parents' absence, before she realised something else sat squashed in the bottom of the box, camouflaged by the remaining tissue.

Reaching in, her fingers brushed over something silky soft, and she lifted up the article. She smiled on seeing a beautiful, midnight blue, knitted hat in what might have been lamb's wool, with the tiniest threads of silver woven through. Just like with the socks, Morgan didn't hesitate in tugging it over her head of yet-to-be-brushed hair. And sat there, feeling subtly contented for a good twenty minutes, while surrounded by items she'd eventually tidy away.

❧

DIPPING the paintbrush into a loosened blob of paint, Morgan scooped up some burnt umber. She had lots of different ways she liked to create a little chaos on the canvas, but today's didn't call for control, and with a forward flick of her arm, the watery substance flicked backward, sideways, forwards, and definitely up and down, all in one stroke. Morgan might even have felt a tiny splat on the tip of her nose, but didn't much care. The painting she'd been working on for weeks was coming to a close, and with just a few more choice colours of spatter and spray, she would call the abstract almost complete. Pearl blue. Raw sienna. Topped with flesh ochre.

Taking her finest brush from the pot, she scooped up some medium to extend the gorgeous indigo she chose next, and moving in close to the artwork, she added the final, fiddly details. If Brandon were there, he'd insist she was finessing the eyes, but as much as the piece had grown more and more to resemble a human, Morgan chose to still be in denial about that. Chose to ignore the slight smile she'd given to the lips, and erratic strokes of colour that could just about, maybe, if one squinted just so, be interpreted as a small flop of hair over a brow. No, siree. She did *not* want to dwell on the complete directness of her painting when she usually applied freedom and little structure to her art.

A loud bleating shook through the room, jolting Morgan enough to cause damage, and she snapped her hand back just in time to save the detail she'd added. She dropped the brush down on the awaiting rag and reached for her phone.

17:30 flashed from the screen, and for a moment, she had absolutely no idea why the phone felt she needed to know.

Until she remembered it was Christmas Eve. And that Sprinkles Of Joy closed in thirty minutes. And that she still hadn't collected the dessert for Christmas dinner with her gran.

That! That was why she'd set an alarm—because she knew damned well she would likely forget once she got caught up in her art room.

Why the heck had she set the alarm with so small a window to spare?

Ignoring the tightening feeling of paint drying on her skin, Morgan half-jogged through to her bedroom, where she tugged her winter boots over her art-crusted jeans, worked a bra on beneath her saggy T-shirt, and topped both of those with the first sweater she grabbed. Make-up, make-up—should she bother? Heck, even a quick wash would've been great, but the ticking time bomb of her phone told her she'd already used up five minutes of her thirty, so she had little choice but to get a wiggle on.

Out by the front door, she yanked on a green-grey fleece

hat with flaps that covered her ears, and shouldered her way into her waterproof after a quick glance through the window showed the day's snow had turned sleety. Then, after scarcely remembering to double back for her bank card, she piled outside into the once-again frigid temperature and onto the street.

Urgh. If there was one thing that haters of snow hated even more weather-wise, it was sleet. At least with snow, which Morgan didn't actually mind that much when she was moving, one could tread their way around the treacherous bits and navigate it at leisure. With sleet? How could a person possibly avoid the fat blobs of partially-frozen wetness that somehow always managed to slide beneath collars, no matter the strive for otherwise, and soaked hair wet through at the same time as coating it in a layer of crusty ice.

Despite the horrid turn in weather, and the early darkness that'd claimed the afternoon, Morgan's street was surprisingly busy. Families popping in last minute to drop off presents and share well-wishes before they celebrated the following day their own way. Bins from that morning's collection being wheeled up front paths by workers who were only just arriving home. The really late starters fixing up decorations, as if they'd just realised they'd forgotten, or had been too busy with life, or had been waiting for the Christmas Eve reductions to buy them.

The comings and goings all felt kind of strange, though, with everyone moving through the shadows. Muted, almost. Or—if her life were a horror movie— even creepy.

Partway down the road, a dark outline moved toward her, morphing into a man with his shoulders hunched as he strode beneath the streetlamp. He glanced up right before swerving a left in through an open gateway, his purposeful pace pausing at the same time as Morgan finally recognised who he was. "How're you doing?" he asked. He never greeted her with a *hi*, or *hello*. Always with a *How are you*, or similar wording. Morgan sometimes wondered if he approached everyone that way, or if there was something about *her* that made him believe she might one day need to spill her woes.

"Hi, Bill," she said, almost slipping to a stop beside his property.

"Lovely weather, this." He nodded up at the sky, squinting as he did so against the the wet onslaught.

Morgan allowed a light laugh. "Depends on who you ask."

"There is that," he agreed. "So, are you ready?"

She didn't have to ask for what. "As I'll ever be."

"Tree up?"

Morgan glanced toward his house, where a six-foot tree stood front and centre in the alcove of the bay window, curtains held aside to ensure passersby could experience the full enthrallment of the display. No gaudy inflatables on the front garden for Bill and his wife. No, siree. Only delicate ornaments decorated their lawn—reindeers woven from willow strands, the tiniest of golden lights illuminating them from the inside out—as classical and classy as the oversized clear baubles on his tree backlit by gold. Morgan didn't have to see the inside of his house to know the rest of his decorations would be to the same standard.

"Not yet," she admitted, before adding, "I'm working on it." Somehow, she smiled through the small lie.

"You'd better get a move on. You only have eight hours left."

"I will," she said. "I promise," she added at his sceptical

expression. She'd just have to work on it once she returned home.

"Well, whether you do, or you don't, have the best of days tomorrow."

"You, too, Bill," she said, and watched him turn away and begin the march up his path, before returning to her journey that suddenly seemed impossible in the time she had left.

Speed-walking over wet and slidey pavements tested Morgan's balance to the max, but with her head down against any other possible greetings, dodging around the *Merry Christmas*'s she hoped were aimed at others and not her when she hadn't time to chat, she finally found herself nearing Chumbrey High Street. At the corner, a car sped past too close to the kerb, and she hopped to the right just in time to avoid being splashed by snow spray. Trying not to curse too much beneath her breath, she let out a sigh of relief on seeing the lights of the bakery still aglow and hearing the sound of the bell over the door as a shadowy figure pushed inside.

As much as she'd dreaded being stuck out on the pavement behind a queue of order collectors, Morgan found the Sprinkles of Joy strangely empty when she entered. Everyone else must've been more organised than herself, preferred to *not* leave jobs to the last minute.

Everyone except the one customer in front of her, anyway.

Blinking against the sudden onslaught of light, she took her place behind the guy who'd beat her inside. From her position, she couldn't see much of him, other than to acknowledge he was tall enough to block out most of her view of Lou behind the counter. And that he'd dressed for the weather in a thick coat, as well as a beanie hat that only allowed a few strands of hair to peek free between that and the hand-knitted, grey scarf wrapped about his neck.

With her hearing taking a moment to adjust to the quiet after the wet and rolling hum of traffic outside, she could only catch a murmur as the guy leaned forward slightly.

"Look, I'm sorry, hun," Lou said as Morgan's ears finally tuned in. "But we just don't give out the details of our customers."

Morgan perked up a little then, checked out the guy's rear-side a bit more thoroughly—though, why, when she couldn't really see any more than she already had, she didn't know.

He must have pulled some kind of face, or pleaded with his eyes, because Lou added, "If I see her, I'll tell her you were looking for her. Now, if you could just …"

He scooted to the left.

Morgan moved forward, but just as she opened her mouth to request her order, the customer ducked his way back in front.

"Sorry," he said with less than even a sideways glance as he leaned over the counter. "Do you have a pen, maybe? And some paper. I could leave a number …"

Morgan froze. Froze as the tone of voice she'd heard bouncing around inside her head for days filled her ears. Froze as Lou reached for a napkin from beneath the counter, slid a pen free of her waistband beneath her apron. She stared at the back of the guy's head, while he took the items then bent low over the counter, his arm angled awkwardly as he wrote, and she tried to pick apart the small details she *could* see. Like the tiny tufts of hair poking out, the broad shoulders, clothing that gave absolutely nothing away because she'd only ever seen him in a work uniform.

As he straightened from the counter, Morgan drank in

his height, and when he turned slightly, she got a profile-glimpse of the face she'd been thinking about for the past week.

Warm eyes beneath a tiny, unruly curl of hair. A mouth she'd seen smiling a couple of times set into a line of disappointment.

"Hiya, flower." Lou switched her focus to Morgan. "You here for your order?"

Morgan nodded, but couldn't quite take her eyes off the man who'd *obviously* come looking.

For *her?*

As if sensing the scrutiny, the guy finally made the full turn toward the door, and as he did so, his gaze caught on her.

Caught between wanting to grin and frown and hide all at the same time, Morgan went with a simple, "Hi."

His shoulders jerked back slightly. His mouth twisted, his eyebrows joining in to create an expression of uncertainty. "Hi."

"I didn't expect to see you here."

"No, me neither." And he truly did look perplexed to be where he was in that moment.

"So, what are you doing here, then?"

His mouth paused slightly ajar, as his eyes flickered to the left, toward where Lou pretended not to be watching their exchange while unfolding a cake box. "I'm ... not sure," he gradually said.

Morgan let out a small laugh at that, before twisting toward the counter just as Lou was closing the lid on a box.

"One Christmas bomb," Lou said, settling it inside a plastic bag she'd pulled out ready. "You know, seeing as I'll need to close at some point today."

Lou's Christmas bombs were about as good as

Christmas dessert could get. A light and fluffy sponge sandwiched around a fresh cream filling, moulded into the shape of a dome and smothered in a freshly made custard, and topped with the finest layer of icing-sugar-dusted marzipan.

"Sorry—thanks, Lou." Morgan tapped her card against the reader to pay.

"And something for the road."

Morgan watched as she set a small package inside the bag, followed by the napkin on which Morgan could see the blue ink Tom had left behind.

"Merry Christmas," Lou said, and handed the bag over with a wink.

"Merry Christmas, Lou." With her hand looped through the bag's handle, Morgan glanced at Tom before nodding toward the door and heading that way.

Back outside, the cold swirled around Morgan as she paused just beyond the bakery and turned to look at the bus driver.

Tom. She really needed to start thinking of him as Tom. Especially with him having turned up at her favourite bakery as if hunting her down.

He'd hunted her down.

Beside them, the snap of a latch sounded out, and she caught Lou in her periphery, locking up shop. She probably should have glanced across fully, sent her a final wave, but she didn't want to see the knowing smile she'd be wearing.

Morgan had enough knowing thoughts of her own with which to contend.

"So …" *Tom* said, standing a good foot taller than her, even with her on her feet.

"So …?" she responded.

In the bakery, when she'd been the one to sneak up on *him*, Morgan hadn't felt quite so wrong footed as she'd imagined she might in such a situation. But outside? In the dark and the cold and with her cover totally blown?

Her only saving grace, really, was that he seemed to have as little clue where to start as she did. He *would* be the one to kick it off, though—especially when he'd been the one to seek *her* out.

As if sensing her intent, he gave a small laugh, and Morgan couldn't help but smile. Even in the small time they'd spent together, she'd grown to understand that his laughter—smiles, even—didn't happen without good cause.

"You're not going to make this easy, are you?" he asked.

"I'm sure I have no idea what you mean." As she spoke, a small shiver worked its way through her body. "But whatever you're here for, we might have to move while you tell me, because it's blooming freezing out here."

"Can I walk you to … you know … wherever it is you're—"

"Home."

He nodded. "Can I walk you home, then? Is tha—"

"Yes."

"Okay." He breathed out what sounded like relief, but neither of them moved immediately.

Warm eyes that glinted in the lamplight stared down at Morgan, above a mouth softened by something she couldn't quite identify. And Morgan she stared right back up at him while doing a shoddy job of disguising the quirk of her lips at it all. At the whole situation. At serendipity and all that nonsense she most definitely didn't believe in.

"Shall we … you know …" He swung his arms a little, breaking Morgan from her wool-gathering, and she jerked away and into a trot back toward the way she'd come.

For minutes, neither spoke. Only the echoing splat of footsteps alongside her own convinced her she really did have an escort back to her flat and it wasn't all just a figment of her rather desperate imagination.

"I was surprised," she said, after a short while. "You know, to see you here. At the bakery."

"To be honest, so was I."

"Why are you, then? Here, I mean."

"Isn't that obvious?"

Her lips curved in the darkness at his obscure admission. "You were cutting it a bit fine, weren't you? The bakery has been open all day, you know."

"Yeah, well, you strike me as more of a spontaneous person than someone who lives life to a plan. The popular breakfast and lunchtime rushes … they wouldn't be your sort of thing."

"And you?"

As a car rolled by, spray arced over the pavement, and he sidestepped behind her to save getting splashed. "Me what?" he asked, rejoining her side.

"Are you spontaneous, or a planner?"

He glanced up, his head tilted slightly to the side. Morgan wished she could see more of his face beneath the scarf he'd pulled up over his chin. "I always thought I was a planner."

"And what changed that?" she asked, turning onto her street.

A quiet pause followed, before he spoke. "Well, it all started with a change in my shift …"

Morgan's lips danced again.

"And this woman who caught my bus."

"George's bus."

"*My* bus that night."

"Okay, okay," she said, waving him on with her hand. "And …?"

"And suddenly I'm sitting staring at the clock on Christmas Eve, with an overwhelming urge to find her like it's my last and only chance."

It took Morgan a few steps to realise he no longer matched her movements, and she turned to see him stopped.

"And there you were," he said simply.

She waited for the laughter that should surely follow, or the shrug of his shoulders like it was crazy or no big deal, or … anything other than the serious expression she found. "There I was," she said quietly.

Again, she found herself simply standing there, simply looking at a man who looked back at her with what seemed as much interest as she herself held. Standing there and staring until the chill wove its way around her ankles and crept along her calves, daring to take a peek beneath the hem of her coat.

Except, that time, she didn't feel any of the earlier awkwardness. Only a heat that belied the temperatures of the ensuing evening.

"This is me," she said, pointing over her shoulder. "Just down here."

"Oh." He didn't move, though.

Neither did she.

"Would you—I dunno. Did you maybe want to get a drink? Or something?"

She frowned. "On Christmas Eve? At this time of day, everyone is either drunk already and realising they've missed the deadline for grabbing last minute presents, so they're deciding they may as well stay because they're already in trouble with their partner. Or they're the kind who planned to stay until they get kicked out anyway."

"You seem to have a lot of insight into people who use pubs on Christmas Eve."

She shrugged with her mouth as much as her shoulders.

"So, that's a no?"

"A definite no."

"Oh." His own shoulders sagged as much as his thick coat would allow, his whole expression seeming to carry what Morgan surmised to be deflation. "Well, it probably wasn't the best timing, my turning up like this on such a busy day."

Goodness, she felt bad at her abruptness, because a *no, go away and leave me alone* vibe *really* wasn't what she'd been aiming for. "It's not busy for me," she told him.

"You probably have a million things to do," he rushed on, like he hadn't heard.

"No, actually," she said, smiling when his body swayed as he finished speaking, as if he'd built himself to walking away and she'd stalled the action with her response. "I just have to decorate my tree." At the reminder, she let out a heavy sigh. Decorating the tree had grown to feel like more of a duty than an enjoyable way to spend an evening, a job she'd dreaded, and hence left to the last minute, for the past two years.

"I could ... help. With that," he said. "If you'd like?"

She lifted her gaze back to his, saw hope in his eyes, a hope she felt inside herself, and although a teeny tiny part her mother had instilled inside of her questioned bringing a guy she knew little of into her home, she also acknowledged the smile creeping back onto her face and the slight sway of her shoulders that said she liked the idea. "Decorating trees *is* more fun with two. Right?"

"Right," he agreed, his head rapidly nodding as if afraid

she might change her mind if he didn't accept the invitation fast enough.

She let out a small laugh. "Okay, then." With a small jerk of her head, she indicated for him to follow as she set back on course. "You'd better come inside."

"Is it warm?"

"Warmer than out here."

A hand she wasn't expecting slipped around her free one. A hand filled with strength and uncertainty all in a single motion. "Count me in, then," he said.

CHAPTER 15

THE LAMPLIGHT INSIDE HER FLAT SUDDENLY SEEMED FAR more exposing to Morgan than the darkness of outside. She became all too aware of the crusted paint across her cheek, the matching smears over her clothing that would be revealed the instant she removed her coat. And all too conscious of the mess Tom would be confronted with as soon as she slipped the hat from her head.

Except, he wasn't even looking her way. Nope, standing just a step in from the doormat, he rubbed his hands together as he glanced from one spot of the room to another. Almost as if his body dealt with as many nerves as her own.

Taking the opportunity for the distraction it was, Morgan quickly shrugged out of her coat, whipped off her hat, and called out, "Back in just a moment," as she darted for the bedroom. Chased by, "Make yourself comfy," the moment she'd rounded the corner.

In the bedroom, she clicked the door to, before leaning back against it and closing her eyes. With heaving flicks of her chest, her breaths battled against her control, and despite her lips shaping around each exhalation, she had little authority over the smile that seemed to be conquering all.

Because Tom was just a door, a wall, a dozen, or so, steps away. In her flat. The bus driver who'd somehow, crazily, caused the first stir in her body and mind she'd had since …

No, she wouldn't be going there. It most certainly wasn't the time.

It *was* time, however, she kicked her arse into gear and made herself look a lot less like the weird eccentric she resembled.

Knowing a complete change of clothing would take far too long and then things would become … well, weird, Morgan grabbed only a clean T-shirt from her drawer. A baggy, oversized number, with splatters of colour surrounding butterflies in flight on its front. Once she'd replaced the paint-hardened one she pulled off, she opened her door a crack and peered outside.

No sign of Tom. No sound of him, either.

Like an intruder in her own home, she tip-toed over the hallway floor and into the bathroom, where she rapid-scrubbed at the colourful crustiness on her face and arms until she'd turned herself a higher shade of radish.

"Not exactly the desired effect," she whispered to herself, but it would have to do.

Shrugging her shoulders up and down a few times, she heaved out a deep breath. Then she ordered herself from the room to face the man she'd–possibly rashly–invited into her home.

And for the first time, standing and staring toward the stretch of living area she could see from her position, she pondered the sensibleness of her decision to just bring someone home with her who was, if she admitted the truth, a stranger.

A stranger. In her flat. With her. Alone.

She found herself shaking her head as she took the first step toward where she'd left him.

Not a stranger. The night bus driver who'd surprised her. In a good way.

Tom.

A shadow of movement shook her free of thought, and she twitched to the left as she snapped her focus to the right.

And there he was. Not where she'd left him at all, but standing in her art room, his head canted to the side, peering at the canvas she hadn't wanted to study too closely since the moment she'd started covering it with paint.

As if realising she'd finally joined him, he made a slow shift of his head, his eyes leading the way until they collided with hers. A slight quirk tugged at his lips. That small flop of hair hung like a question mark over his brow.

She found herself smoothing her hands over jeans softened by days of wear, and wondered if she should have made more of an effort. Because Tom had removed his hat. His scarf. His coat. And underneath, the soft knitted jumper he wore moulded over a broad chest and defined shoulders, curling slightly at its hem where it met a just-right waist. His jeans, not too tight, not too loose, somehow managed to show off muscular thighs on their route to heavy-tread boots.

He straightened a little more from his stance, and Morgan realised she might have stared for a fraction too long—or possibly a whole decimal point of too much time.

She worked her mouth around an awkward, "Hi."

"Did you paint this?" he asked, his finger prodding toward the art.

She had. She totally had. And while she was so very proud of that fact, the way she felt proud any time she completed a new piece, she really didn't want him staring at it any longer. Not because he might be on side with Brandon and see something in the painting that simply wasn't there, no siree, but because …. Well, just because.

"I'll make us a drink," she said, and jerking her head for him to follow, she made for the kitchen.

"It's good," he said behind her. "Really good."

"Thanks," she muttered.

"It's a man, right?"

She didn't reply as she busied herself filling the kettle and flicking it on.

"Is it your … you know. Your guy?"

She paused with a couple of mugs in her hand, a frown tugging at her face. No, the artwork looked nothing like Philip. The face in the painting resembled someone else completely.

Lowering the cups to the counter, she gave a gentle shake of her head. "No, it's not Philip."

The poor guy's chin lifted like he felt he'd just made a terrible faux pas, and he buried his hands into the pockets of his jeans. "Sorry."

"Don't be," she said, half turning toward where he leaned against the doorframe. "It's okay." And as she said the words, she realised it was. That the whole situation was okay. *She* was okay. Having Tom standing in her kitchen with her was more than okay. So, why on earth was she acting like a rigid idiot whose batteries were about to run dead. "Is hot chocolate okay?" She shook the canister at him. "There's just something about coming in from the snow that calls for hot chocolate."

He seemed to hesitate for a moment, before asking, "Are you still cold?"

Morgan breathed out a small laugh and glanced away. "Not since you followed me into my flat." She dared to peer back at him. "I don't feel cold at all."

There it was. That smile of his. He'd shown only a preview of it in the bedroom, like a sneaky peek at the head-liner he shared with her right then. Goodness, that burning in her chest could only be a good thing, right? A warmth that blossomed outward into her shoulders and danced in clogs through her belly.

Beside her, the kettle hissed and spewed steam, and as the switch clicked itself off, the pot quit vibrating. Letting her hair fall forward around her heated cheeks, she spooned powder into the mugs, concentrated on holding her hand steady enough for pouring boiling water.

"It's the first time I've seen you without a hat," he said, from the doorway.

A reminder that Morgan hadn't tidied her blooming hair. For goodness sake, she probably looked like Medusa's second cousin twice-removed–whatever that meant. It took all her efforts to resist patting it down right there in front of him.

"Your hair—"

Okay, she totally needed to pat it down.

"No, don't," he said, taking a half-step toward her as she tugged at the strands. "It looks fine." He smiled. Again. Making her insides celebrate again. "More than fine, actually."

"Thanks," she said, stirring the spoon like crazy to save her embarrassment being on full display. Swinging round on the spot, she almost flung the mugs his way as she nodded toward the lounge. "Shall we?"

"Oh, er … sure." With so little space in the kitchen, he backed himself into the lounge, and Morgan followed him in.

She'd wondered for a very brief second where he might sit, half-dreaded and half-hoped he'd take the armchair to create some space, but no. Tom sank himself down on her slightly-worn and much-loved sofa, his knees bending high to accommodate his new position and his elbows hitting his thighs as he twisted to see where she'd go. It was interesting body language to see, for a woman long out of the dating game, dealing with the moves people made. Code for, *Here I am, I'm being respectful, the next move is on you.*

And maybe, for the briefest of moments, Morgan did contemplate taking the armchair, creating distance, curling her knees up against her chest and creating a barrier against any hurts she didn't even know would come, but ….

She realised in just as brief an instant that she'd much rather be sitting right next to the handsome guy who filled her living room with his presence. So she did.

"For you," she said, holding out one of the mugs.

He took the drink from her, and she could've sworn he manipulated the brush of their fingers as he did so. Forcing herself not to twitch, or shiver, or fall victim to any of the sensations trying to take over at the contact, she reached for her own mug and clinked it against his. A meagre attempt at hiding her feelings.

"Cheers." She blurted the word a little too eagerly, but if he noticed her awkwardness, it didn't show. Probably because she'd been awkward since the moment they'd first spoken, so why should he expect anything less?

Sipping on her too-hot chocolate drink, she tried not to watch the casual way he sat, the cup held loosely in his hand like some kind of prop, rather than a beverage to actually be drunk, or the slow swivel of his head as he no doubt took in his untidied surroundings.

"I'm guessing that's the tree," he said, and Morgan followed his gaze toward its beaten and battered box, covered in tattered strands of sellotape from years of being packed away. It'd been her parents' tree before they'd moved away, and her gran's for a short while, before being handed down once again.

Inwardly cringing, she tipped her head with an embarrassed smile. "'Fraid so."

"Did you want to …?"

But she didn't get a chance to answer whatever question he meant to pose, because Tom had already climbed to his feet and was rounding the table he'd placed his cup on, toward the half-drunk box in the corner. Blasted article looked like it'd had too much port with its cheese.

Grabbing it up, he breathed out a quiet laugh. "Looks as bad as Mum's."

"I feel like I'm supposed to apologise for that …"

"Never," he said, meeting her eyes and jellyifying her stomach. "Anything that looks this much of a relic and still gets used must be loved."

"Or I just can't be bothered to fork out for a new one." *For a celebration I don't much like*, she didn't add.

"Or that." He gave the box a small shake in her direction. "Shall we—you want—"

"Yes," Morgan said, setting down her cup and standing. It almost felt as though she'd been awaiting permission to move. Not from Tom, though—she knew that much. Maybe she needed permission from herself, and Tom taking the first step had given her the kick she'd needed. "I'll grab some scissors."

She found the scissors in the kitchen drawer they'd

always lived in, and carried them through to where Tom waited and waved them at him with a smile.

"Do the honours," he said, angling the box just so, and Morgan leaned in, ordering her tongue to stay inside her mouth as she made the first cut.

With the incision made, the box gaped just enough to show a glimpse of the dark green spininess inside. "One down, about forty billion to go."

Tom released a low chuckle that set her nape hairs ruffling. "It's okay, I've got all night."

For the briefest of moments, Morgan drank in those words, her brain analysing and over-analysing far too quickly for her thoughts to keep up, but before the madness could take over, she pushed it all aside. He didn't mean anything by it. It wasn't an innuendo. Not a self-invitation, nor an advertisement of availability.

One snip of brittle tape became two, then three, and on the fourth cut, halfway along the box's seam, a thudding of heads had Morgan glancing up on a laugh. But that laughter eased the moment she realised how close their heads had actually grown, how close to his face her own suddenly was, and the depth of expression staring back at her from his eyes. Before she had chance to question his thoughts, or her own, he ducked his face closer, popped the gentlest of kisses on the very edge of her lips, and drew back again as though afraid to overstay his welcome into her personal space.

And didn't that just send her brain into overdrive, and the lips he'd just kissed into the wonkiest of smiles. A sudden shyness had her glancing away. "We haven't even got the tree out of the box yet."

A low bark of laughter drew her gaze back up, and what a wonderful sight to behold, those eyes of his filled with amusement and warmth, until Morgan found herself laughing right alongside him.

"Seriously, though," she said, still grinning.

"Right." He nodded, although his mirth remained. "Concentrate."

So she did, using the distraction of getting the damned box open to avert her lips from returning to his and rushing into a full-on snog that might land her where she wasn't yet sure she'd be ready to go.

With the last slice of tape broken, the tree sprang free, flicking dust and glitter into the air, and dropping loose fronds of green onto the rug. Tom set about assembling the trunk without instruction, so Morgan pieced together the base, and as though working through some unspoken routine they'd done a hundred times, or more, they connected their two pieces together and stood the sorry tree on its feet.

"Perfect," Tom said, and Morgan elbowed him in his side.

"Don't make fun of my tree. It—"

"Needs chucking in the bin?"

"Holds a lot of memories, actually."

A quiet followed, and she got the impression *he* was suddenly the one trying to evaluate her words. Wondered if he rolled through what memories those might be.

"It belonged to my parents'," she said. "It's almost as old as me."

"I've got to say, you've worn much better that it has."

Staring at the darned thing, with a couple of branches missing and whole lot more of its fake needles gone to the grave, she wasn't sure how much of a compliment that could be considered. "Wait until you see the baubles," she muttered.

He laughed. Again. The sound that'd once felt like an achievement not so very long ago, suddenly felt like a natural presence in her home. "Can hardly wait."

"Well, they're only in that other box there ..."

"I can take the hint," he said, and stepped over to grab the box up. "Oh, good. More excessive tape." Back beside the coffee table, he lowered the box down, pecking another gentle kiss to her cheek before releasing it. "Pass the scissors, and I'll do the deed."

"Worried about your precious head?"

He peered up at her from his bent position, an unreadable gleam in his eyes. "Not even a little bit." He held out his hand, and she passed him the scissors from where she'd laid them on the armchair.

Taking a step back, she watched as he slid one scissor blade through each taut swatch of tape, marvelling at how such a small and simple task could somehow accentuate the curves of the muscles in his arms and shoulders. She was still staring when he unveiled the box's contents with a grin.

"You first," he said.

She blinked, confused for a moment by his words, until he lifted out a threadbare bauble and let it dangle between them.

"It *is* your tree."

Breathing out a soft laugh, Morgan took the embarrassing article from him and, after wrangling a branch into a passable pose, positioned it in place.

"You weren't kidding about the state of these baubles," he said, eyeing up the next one he passed, one that should've been bright greens and reds, but had faded to ugly salmon pink and dirty greys.

"I rarely kid."

"About anything?"

She turned to see a single eyebrow arched high enough to meet his curl of hair. Adorable. "Except my weight, my height. Sometimes my age."

"All of which are already perfect."

She barked out a loud guffaw—not exactly impressive material—and slapped a hand over her mouth in an effort to catch it. "You don't even know how old I am."

"I don't even know your name," he countered.

"Oh!" Her rounded mouth stayed there for a moment. She could've sworn she'd given it to him, aside from her attempted yell at the closing bus doors. And she'd have sworn he must've heard her, considering she'd screamed it loud enough to wake the entire street. "Well, then ..." She held out her hand. "Morgan King. Nice to meet you."

He took her hand, held it softly within his own as he stared down at her. "Tom—"

"I know."

He tipped his head to the side, as if trying to figure out how she knew, but she merely shrugged.

"I have good contacts."

He relaxed into a smile. "George."

"A girl never divulges ..." She tapped the side of her nose.

"Well, it's nice to *finally* meet you, too." And digging into the box of relics, he tugged out another horrific decoration and handed it over. "Next."

CHAPTER 16

BITS OF TINSEL LITTERED THE FLOOR, AMID BAUBLES EVEN Morgan had to admit didn't cut the mark. It had taken a broken string, or more inner plastic than threads showing, for her to admit they just might finally need discarding, though.

Pausing to view their handwork, Morgan took a bite of an exceptional mince pie, the pastry so soft and buttery it all but melted in her mouth. "Mmm, Lou really outdid herself with these."

"I would answer …" Tom stared down at his own mince pie like an adoring puppy at its owner. "But I'm having a moment."

A laugh erupted from Morgan, and she whipped her hand up to snare any crumbs before they could explode from her mouth. After coughing on an errant dot of sugar, she dared lower her hand back down again. "Now you know why it's my favourite bakery."

"I think it might be mine, too, now."

"And this is why we were destined to meet."

Smile aimed one-hundred percent at his pastry, he smiled.

"Too much?"

"Not even by a smidgen."

The discarded paper bag from the pies sat in a crumpled mound on the coffee table, next to half-empty mugs of their second hot chocolate. Focusing on those helped Morgan to control the crazy grin her lips tried forming, as she fed the rest of her pie into her mouth and chewed.

Beside her, Tom dusted his hands together, before picking crumbs from his 'Roam Wild' T-shirt and popping them into his mouth like he couldn't bear to waste even a speck. His jumper had come off a half-hour earlier—something Morgan had been very happy to witness, even if she hadn't fully admitted it to herself.

"Not much left," he said.

Morgan lifted her food-empty hands. "Nothing left, actually."

"I meant the tree," he said, nodding toward it.

In truth, there were plenty more baubles—her parents had always gone overboard, as if they couldn't stand for a single branch to be bare—but they just weren't really fit for use anymore. Actually, none of the decorations had much life left in them, but Morgan never had been very good at letting go. Even the sorry lot they'd tossed aside as *too* far gone would likely end up back in the box rather than the bin.

She picked up one yet to be evaluated. "Better get to it, then."

Tom wiggled his loosely-held fist. "Ding-ling-ling. Round two." He scooped up three baubles in one hand. "You do realise nobody else on the planet has this many things on their tree, don't you?"

"I'll bet rich people do."

"Yeah, but rich people have bigger trees. Hence more room to put them."

"Are you telling me ..." She twisted toward him with a turned-grey cotton ball held up between them. "You've been in my home for ... how long?" She had no idea. "Anyway— you're only just mentioning *now* that you don't like my tree?"

"But if I like *you*, doesn't that kind of counter the .... Well, I wouldn't exactly call it a *dislike*. More ..." His nose scrunched in a really cute way Morgan totally didn't notice. "More a doubt in its ability to perform."

"Hmmph."

"It's like, when really old pop bands can't seem to quit singing, but they just don't sound the same anymore, no matter how much they want to think otherwise."

"Right."

"Or when people too stuck in their ways to change keep the same sofa, or bed, for thirty years, without realising it's so full of mites and dust that it's probably slowing killing them."

"Extreme, much."

"Sometimes it takes an extreme explanation for an extreme person."

She frowned. "You think I'm extreme?" She wasn't sure that sounded very much like a compliment.

"You are."

She folded her arms across her chest.

"Extremely different," he said.

She narrowed her eyes, but he ducked closer.

"Extremely unique."

Her eyes eased up a little.

"Dare I say extremely cute?"

"Just cute?

"And beautiful."

He bridged the remaining gap until his lips met hers in a soft, lingering kiss that had her fingers reaching up to brush his jaw.

"You're extremely forgiven," she murmured as he drew back slightly.

"Thought that might do it." With a wink, he held up an angel who looked like she'd spent her life working on the streets. "Anyway, I found this lurker in the box. Wouldn't happen to know her, would you?"

Smiling, she swiped her beloved 'fairy' free of his hand. "Show some respect. She's an antique, I'll have you know."

"A relic, you say?"

"Oi!" She elbowed him in the ribs and turned toward the tree.

As a toddler, she'd been lifted into the air by one of her parents until her little arms had been high enough to plant the angel. And as a child and pre-teen, they'd brought in the step-stool for her to climb high enough herself.

Since then, she'd been stretching herself on tiptoes, teetering as she positioned the final piece, but as she did exactly that right then, a warm pair of hands cupped her hips, and heat spread across her back as he moved closer.

"Go on, I've got you."

Swallowing down a stuttered breath, Morgan gripped one of his hands like she needed that extra ounce of steadying, and set her childhood memory astride the tallest spike of tree. As she lowered back to her soles, though, his hands didn't move. He didn't step away. Her shoulders bumped his chest. And she stood there for a moment, unsure what to do—or *questioning* her next move, at least. Was she supposed to be the one to break the hold? Or did he expect her to turn around? The way his breaths deepened above her ear said he quite liked the position they'd found themselves in, and maybe, just maybe, he wanted more. But as if he needed the decision to be hers, he didn't shift, or push, or try twisting her to face him.

She should face him, though. Least of all because she really, really wanted to.

Taking a deep breath, she set her resolve, and—

Her mobile phone blared through the room, and she jolted herself free of his soft grip.

"Sorry," she said, a laugh breaking free around the word. For the briefest of moments, she considered ignoring the ringing … until she remembered who it would likely be. "Oh, what time—I should probably …" She snuck from his cocoon and, after a moment of chasing the sound, pulled her phone from where she'd left it, in her coat pocket, and hit 'Answer'.

"Hello?"

"Ah, there you are."

"I'm so sorry, Gran."

"There's no need to—"

"I didn't realise the time." She paused with a frown, before asking, "What time *is* it?"

"Never mind that. I just wanted to make sure you were all right."

"Sorry, Gran. I have no idea what—I must have lost track—."

"For goodness sake, stop apologising. You're not beholden to me."

"Well, I know, but …"

"If you're not here yet, and nothing bad has happened, then it must be something important holding you up."

She glanced toward where Tom had begun fitting the too-far-gone baubles back into their box, and couldn't help but smile at the realisation that he somehow knew she wouldn't be able to part with them just yet, even if they had been retired from duty. "Yes, quite important," she said into the phone."

Tom held up a nutcracker with no arms and his face half missing where the original paint had worn away. His eyebrows danced out his question as he pointed at the sorry article with a shrug of his shoulder, and Morgan laughed before she even realised she was going to. Before she had chance to remember she was still in a call.

"What has you so tickled?" her gran asked.

"Oh!" She darted her gaze from Tom in an effort to regain control. "Just ... something."

"Or maybe you have company?"

"Oh, er ..."

"Would you like me to call back later?"

"Well, I'll be at yours later, Gran, won't I?"

"You know, you can always leave coming over here until tomorrow. If you need to."

"I couldn't do that."

"Well, if you have other plans ..."

And suddenly there it was. The *knowing* tone in her gran's voice. Morgan wasn't sure if being twigged was a good thing, or a bad thing. Considering the inquisition she'd likely face, if not on arrival at her gran's, then definitely in the morning, maybe it leaned more toward the latter. Even so ... "I'll be there," she assured her gran. She hadn't left her grandmother stranded on Christmas Eve yet—not since her parents had migrated—and it wasn't something she intended to do then.

"But you know you don't *have* to."

"Okay, listen ..." She paused as Tom folded the flaps over the repacked, damaged decorations and lifted the box.

"Where should I …?" he whispered.

Shaking her head, she waved for him to leave it. "Tonight, I …" she said into the phone before not really knowing how to explain it all, so she went with, "This evening was most … unexpected." Tom grinned in a way that had her own lips responding. "But I'll be there. Because I want to, not because I have to," she tacked on the end.

"I hate to think I'm coming in the way of any fun you might be having," her gran said.

For a moment, Morgan actually paused to consider the fun she could continue to have, should she not head out into the cold that evening. But those thoughts led to the alternative, and the warmth she'd stay cooped up in, instead, and then the heat that staying in the warmth could quite possibly lead to. Finally landing on the realisation that, as much as she'd loved Tom showing up in search of her, and having taken the leap to invite him into her home, which had led to a lovely, lovely evening … she really needed to take whatever was happening between her and the bus driver she'd only recently met much slower than that.

No, staying home and seeing where the evening went should wait for another, more surer time.

Assuming there'd be one.

"I'll *be* there," she repeated, her voice a little firmer.

"I'm holding you up," Tom said once she'd said her goodbyes to her gran.

She winced slightly. "As much as I want to say *no* …"

He waved her off.

"And as much as I *really* would be quite happy to contin-ue"—she circled her hands—"*this* …"

"It's too much, too soon."

"Well, I wouldn't have worded it quite like that."

He grinned. "It's fine. Really." His smile lessened a little when he asked, "How soon do you need to leave?"

Morgan lifted her phone and illuminated the screen, double blinking at the time. "Oh, wow. It's after nine."

"What time should you have left?"

"I usually get to Gran's around eight."

"Soon, then," he said, and as much as he smiled, she detected a hint of sadness in his voice. A sadness she felt within herself, despite knowing she was making the right decision. "I could–I could drive you. If you like?"

She half smiled, half frowned. "You don't have a car."

"Actually, I do. How else did you think I got here?"

"I don't know. By bus?"

"On Christmas Eve? That'd be pretty presumptuous of me, don't you think–considering getting buses any time after teatime tonight would have been …"

"Close to impossible?" she asked.

"Yeah, that."

"And you're a bus driver."

He laughed.

"So, your car is …?"

"It's over near the bakery."

"Ah."

"To be honest, I never really expected to see you." He shrugged. "Despite, you know?"

"But you came anyway."

"Because you'll never know, if you never try."

"So, are you glad you did?"

His face did that thing she'd noticed in him, where it transformed in an instant. Where any worry lines faded away, to be replaced with softness and warmth, and illumination as a smile worked its way in. "Yeah."

"Good," she said, her expression matching his.

After too many seconds of her silently swooning and bordering on creepy, he asked, "So, shall I?"

"Huhm?"

"Get the car?"

"Oh. Well, yes," she said, grinning. "That would be lovely."

CHAPTER 17

IT HADN'T TAKEN MORGAN LONG TO THROW SOME CLOTHES into a small suitcase. The same pyjamas she'd worn the previous year, in greens and yellows, with a big, red *Ho, ho ho!* on their front. She'd also tossed in the requisite seasonal outfit–requisite simply because it made her gran *ooh* and *aah* and smile to the hills. Her newest one consisted of a swing dress in a fabric printed with a traditional village snow scene, shire-horse-drawn carriage to boot, and a pair of bright green tights for her legs. Really, she should've made the effort to dress up for her arrival, but with the time whirring on, she'd merely pulled on her boots and coat, and topped them with the new winter woolly from her parents.

"Nice car," she'd said with a smile, when Tom had returned with it.

Even the soft glow of the street lamp couldn't disguise the small Fiat 500, like a bubble of white amid the greying snow. Morgan had expected something … well, bigger? It felt like a weird oxymoron seeing Tom behind the Fiat's wheel after seeing him surrounded by a huge block of bus in comparison. His seeming to unfold himself from the driver's seat hadn't helped, either.

"Nice hat," Tom had said in comeback, and the remark had sparked an entire conversation about the received parcel and her parents' lifestyle, and how she missed them at the same time as having grown accustomed to their absence.

Before she knew it—before she was ready—they'd completed the almost four-mile journey, and he was following her directions into her gran's cul-de-sac.

"Which one is it?" Tom asked, slowing to a stop at the mouth of the road.

"I'll give you a clue," Morgan said with a smile. "She's my complete opposite and is probably the most organised in the street."

"I have to guess?"

"If you can."

"Oookay. Challenge accepted." The wink he sent across set Morgan's stomach a-flutter, before he gently rolled over the tarmac between the bungalows.

Not an awful lot set each property aside from its neighbours. Except for one thing—and Morgan wondered if it would guide him as easily as the North Star had the wise men.

The car stopped moving, and he twisted toward her. "This one?"

"Are you asking, or guessing?"

"Guessing. I'm pretty sure it's this one."

"Why?" she asked, a grin growing across her lips.

"Well … that!" He pointed toward the garden outside his window—namely at the huge *Noel* dominating the front lawn, in the way it completely filled the width of the grass and, in all its five-foot glory, flashed and sparkled like a possessed glitter ball at a disco. "Am I right?"

Letting loose a quiet laugh, Morgan climbed from the car, answering only as she reached into the back, where she'd placed the collected cake for safe keeping. "You are."

His door opened as she straightened, and Tom met her at the rear of the vehicle, where he'd stowed her suitcase and small bag of gifts for her gran. "I'll help you with these."

"Thanks," she said, suddenly nervous about saying goodbye. Well, not exactly saying it, more *how* to say it. Like the ridiculous routines at the end of a first date, where one never knew how forward or reserved to act, because either one, if the wrong one, could leave a person feeling like a buffoon. Morgan really didn't want to feel like a buffoon.

And she was overthinking again.

Shaking her thoughts loose, she reached for the handle of her case at the same time as Tom, their fingers brushing and noses almost touching.

"You don't have to carry everything on your own," he said quietly, almost as though his words meant more than they didn't. "Let me help."

"You make me sound like a charity case."

"Not even close."

She studied his too-close eyes for a moment longer. His unwavering stare. "Okay," she said, and releasing her hold on the case, she reached for the bag of gifts instead, glancing across at him as he guided the wheels across the paved footpath beside her.

The front door of her gran's bungalow opened before they reached it, and her gran stood silhouetted by the hallway light that shone so brightly, Morgan felt as though an inquisition might be forthcoming and the torturing had already begun.

"I'm fine, Gran," she said before any words could be

uttered. "Go back inside where it's warm."

"I didn't realise you'd be bringing company." Her gran's voice held zero annoyance, but an abundance of curiosity.

"Oh, it's not like that," Morgan said, hoping beyond hope that she wouldn't be asked to explain just why she'd turned up with a stranger in tow, when she was still processing the whole evening herself.

Two strides forward took Tom into the light of the hall-way, and rounding the suitcase he'd wheeled, he held out his hand. "Nice to meet you."

Her gran held a hand just out of reach and arched a well-sculpted eyebrow until Tom seemed to get the message she broadcasted.

"I'm Tom," he added with a nod, and the two of them shook, before her gran pulled her housecoat together around her shoulders.

"Very nice to meet you, young man. Will you be joining us?"

"Oh, er." Tom sent a nervous glance Morgan's way before shaking his head. "Thank you, but I have some things to take care of myself."

"Well, that's a shame. Shall I take that for you?" she asked, turning toward Morgan, and before she could protest, the cake box vanished from her hand and her gran retreated into the house, pushing the door closed just enough to give the two of them some privacy.

"Subtle, my gran," Morgan said with a small shrug, and Tom laughed.

"I like her."

"Most people do."

He opened his mouth as though to speak again, but closed it just as fast. Morgan knew how he felt. Standing on her doorstep in the dark, the goodbye they needed to share taking up space between them. The questions they needed to ask still unspoken. Even kicking the toes of her boots against the paving didn't distract from the decision she—they—needed to make.

"So …" Tom said, speaking first.

"So …" Morgan responded.

"I had a good time tonight."

"Me, too."

"Would you, maybe—"

"Yes."

He nodded, glanced down toward where Morgan ground her toes against the slabs. "You have my number." He peered back up at her. "I think, anyway—it was in the bakery bag …"

"It was. Louise can be—"

"Shrewd?"

Morgan tinkled out a laugh. "Yeah."

"Okay, then …" Reaching out, his hand, warmer than she'd expected, cupped the side of her cheek, and a moment later, he leaned his lips closer until they pressed against hers.

And goodness, it took everything in her willpower not to grip hold of his coat and drag him in tighter, to hold him captive until she'd been kissed breathless. It was the artist in her, the wanting to act impulsively while hoping mistakes could be fixed at a later date. Thankfully, her gran's level headedness she'd inherited often elbowed its way past and took control of the situation, as it did right then.

Ending the kiss before it had barely gotten started, he rested his forehead against the rim of her hat, before lifting away altogether and creating a crack into which the cold seeped. "Goodnight, Morgan King. I hope you have a lovely Christmas."

And with that, he turned and walked away.

CHAPTER 18

By Christmas dinnertime, Morgan's gran had only mentioned the 'gentleman from last night' about forty-five times. Maybe even more than that. And as much as Morgan had tried to distract her, none of it had worked. As usual, her gran hadn't even indulged in any gift opening yet—not at breakfast, or lunch, and not since they'd forced down a slice of the exquisite dessert cake on top of their meal. Nor had she allowed Morgan to … just in case.

Just *in case* her parents remembered to call. Just *in case* they didn't let them down, as they had on more than one occasion. Some years, Morgan and her gran didn't hear from them until New Year's Day—and only that call came later in the afternoon once they'd slept off any shenanigans they'd gotten up to the night before. Almost as if they spent the entire season celebrating, and completely forgot through all their fun and frolics that they had a parent and child back in England.

Thankfully, it wasn't going to be one of *those* years. Four minutes before, Morgan's tablet had started chirping, and she'd raced to answer the call at her gran's insistence that she 'be quick in case they hang up'.

From the screen, two heavy-eyed and tanned faces smiled sleepily out at them. "And then Brenda said, *Do we get a discount for bulk?* So, everyone got them this year," her mum finished with a chuckle, after a two-minute explanation of why both Morgan and her gran had ended up with the same hat in their boxes.

Which was a shame for her gran, considering she hadn't even opened hers yet. It would take her parents to stop talking long enough for that to happen.

"I have no idea what she's even talking about," said her dad, and Morgan rolled her eyes. Her dad seemed to spend most of his life in his own clueless little bubble, only popping out of it to smile dreamily and drink wine.

"I showed them to you," her mum said, before shrugging her eyebrows at the screen. "For goodness sake, you'd better show them to him."

"Sounds like present opening time," Morgan muttered. "*Finally.*"

"Patience is a virtue, dear," her gran said, as Morgan lifted her gran's box to place down between the coffee table and sofa where the two of them sat.

"I already opened mine," Morgan said.

"Of course you did, pudding," her dad said with a wonky smile. "How's your art going?"

"I just finished a piece this week."

"Will you show it to me?"

"Well, I can't right now, Dad. It's at home, and I'm here, aren't I?"

"But when you get home. Will you send me a photo on that app thing you use?"

"Maybe," Morgan said, as her gran pulled the first item

out of her box, and she glanced down to see what else she had in there.

Olive oil, cookies, pastelles and palmeritas …. Maybe hats hadn't been the only thing her mother had bought in bulk.

"So, what's happening in the world of Morgan?" her mum asked, like she'd already grown bored of watching the gift unwrapping.

Morgan thought back to the evening before. To warm eyes and floppy hair and a Christmas tree that looked about as sad and old as it was, yet somehow a little bit more interesting than it had before. "Nothing, really," she said.

"A new man," her gran said at the same time, and Morgan wanted to groan and shut down the call before the questions could happen. She didn't even have time to hope her parents hadn't heard the comment, because two sets of eyebrows shot up and a sudden spark of interest shone out at her.

"I don't have a new man," Morgan said with a shake of her head.

"That must have been a taxi you were in last night, then," her gran said. "And the driver who got out to say goodbye to you. And the reason you were late."

"You were late?" her parents said together, as though she'd performed some serious insult to the way things should be.

"Not *that* late," she muttered. "Not as late as your call last year." Four days late, that one had been.

"Because you were with a man?" her dad asked, like she hadn't just tried to turn it back on them.

"Who is he?" her mum asked.

"No idea," her gran said. "She still hasn't told me."

146

Her mum's gaze switched side to side before settling back on Morgan. "He must be someone special, then."

"I only just met him," Morgan said.

"Ha!" her mum said, to her dad's: "So, there *is* someone?"

"I swear I'm the only person I know who has to put up with multiple inquisitions over guys."

"You don't *have guys*," her mum said. "That's the whole point."

"Oh, I love these," her gran said beside her, holding up a pair of socks exactly like the ones Morgan had received.

"They're really warm," Morgan assured her.

"You're changing the subject," her mum said.

"Yes," Morgan said with a nod. "Yes, I am."

ॐ

THE PHONE CALL with her parents had lasted only ten minutes more, once they'd accepted she wouldn't be feeding them gossip—not about herself, anyway. They hadn't even stuck around for the rest of the gifts, but Morgan didn't mind. She quite liked the intimacy of exchanging them when it was just herself and her gran. Quite liked when she could hug whatever she received to her chest without having to show it off—because her gran always knew exactly what to buy. Art supplies and underwear. One, because she knew exactly what company she liked for her supplies, and two because she'd never have any 'nice' underwear, or matching sets, if not for the replacement stock her gran ensured she had every year.

And her gran had been super impressed with the comfy headphones Morgan had bought for her, so she could watch all her favourite shows out in the conservatory without disturbing the neighbours. And the requisite annual dressing gown and slippers.

While Christmas Day with Gran had been as warming as it always had been, Morgan felt utterly exhausted. Utterly contented. And utterly frustrated. All in equal measures.

Yes, the day had been everything she'd come to expect and looked forward to, yet … as much as she'd tried to push the previous evening to the back of her mind, the uncertainty of where she and Tom might 'be going', that all-too-abrupt parting … the eddy of thoughts had spiralled through her brain amid all the festivities. And the fact she walked the route home, her suitcase packed with the addition of gifts and a plastic bag filled with leftovers—because her gran never believed she ate enough—only seemed to drive home the vast difference between the two days.

Gran's next door neighbour Mr Dewsbury had, as always, offered to drive her, and even if she didn't always gracefully bow out because it was Christmas and she didn't like to drag him out on such a day, it would have felt wrong returning to her flat in a car filled with awkward small talk, especially after the journey on the way there had been filled with so much … well, hope, she supposed.

"I hope you're going to call him," her gran had whispered as they'd hugged their goodbyes—which meant she hadn't stepped away very far after giving them privacy, the night before, if she'd managed to earwig that much.

"I'm thinking about it," Morgan had assured her.

Only trouble was, she couldn't *stop* thinking about it. And thinking about it. And overthinking to the point of twisting her own thoughts into reasons why she shouldn't because maybe she'd misinterpreted the whole event, made the evening out to be so much better in her mind than it actually was. Three-and-a-half miles of walking was plenty of time for the brain to drive its owner crazy, after all.

"Oh, shut up," she mumbled at herself, as she dragged her wheels over a particularly difficult lump of snow. She'd about had enough of listening to herself for one day.

Maybe getting out her art supplies would help quell the noise.

Morgan turned onto the quietness of her street. On a dryer, warmer Christmas Day, the street might have been claimed by the local kids trying out any new outdoor toys. Bikes, skateboards, footballs, and the like. On a wintry day like that one, unless she happened to cross the front of a home just as visitors arrived or left, the place seemed deserted. Deserted and quiet, and a little bit sad, because half of the properties had forgone lighting up their windows and gardens, as if the festivities had gotten in the way.

Ten more metres to go, Morgan trudged her way to her footpath, her legs beginning to tire and her arm already aching. Her legs freezing through the tights she wore beneath her seasonal dress.

She rounded the gateway to the property, twisting to drag her case through after her and grunting against the effort, but the second she turned back toward the path, she stopped in her tracks.

For there, right on the doormat outside her door, sat a small, square box wrapped in green tissue paper and ensconced in a thick, golden ribbon that'd been tied in a bow to top everything off.

Morgan stared down at it as she moved closer. Stared down at it as she fiddled out her keys and unlocked her door. Stared as if it might just disappear, should she dare remove her eyes from the incongruous article. Maybe she should've been hoping for it to do exactly that, actually–it could have been anything in the box, after all.

Yet, something told her nothing bad hid inside. And the stirrings of excitement bubbled in her tummy, that sliver of anticipation one got at receiving something they hadn't been expecting, and they weren't sure whether to prolong the feeling, or just rip their way inside out of impatience.

Morgan found herself somewhere in the middle of that quandary.

Not wanting to be too hasty, she made sure to lift her case over the box and into the apartment first. To remove her coat and hat and scarf and hang them up. To kick off her boots, which she left just behind the door.

Only then did she collect the mystery package from her doorstep, and after closing herself in for the evening, she carried it through to the kitchen and gently placed it down on the counter, intermittently peering its way while she tidied away the leftovers her gran had given her into the fridge.

For a moment, she considered torturing herself further. Leaving it where it was while she got changed into something more comfortable. Maybe she would have done, if the light hadn't caught the parcel just so as she turned, and set the tips of the ribbon sparkling so brightly, she had little chance of ignoring it any longer.

"Fine," she said, gathering it up and carrying it through to the sofa. "But only because I think you've been dropped at the wrong door and I might need to redeliver you."

As if talking to a wrapped box was the most normal thing in the world, Morgan gave a smug nod at her thought process and pulled on the ribbon, surprised when the single tug unravelled the entire strand in one inning and it dropped to her lap. Well, that had been easier than she'd

THE NIGHT BUS BEFORE CHRISTMAS

expected. Whenever her gran had dressed gifts in ribbon, it had always taken minutes of untying knots that required teeth work as well as fingers. Probably why her gran hadn't used ribbon in a while.

The tissue paper came away equally as easily, and Morgan found herself studying a plain, brown box made of unsubstantial cardboard. Obviously, curiosity had her lifting the flap and peering inside, and the moment her gaze alighted on its content, her head tipped a little to the side, her eyes narrowed just the tiniest bit, and a ghost of a smile joined in on her bemusement.

Inside the box, topped with a fine, red ribbon, sat a perfectly-blown bauble made of glass. Further staring produced the certainty that the glass orb held something, and it wasn't until she drew it up out of its confines that she could see what it was. Or that she could see the small slip of notepaper beneath. Switching the bauble for the paper, she opened the note to slightly scrawly and slanted handwriting.

I found this in a Christmas shop a couple years back
Figured your tree needed it more than mine
x

Morgan laughed at the note before retrieving the bauble once more, warmth spreading through her entire body at the kind and lovely gesture. For within the bauble, as if floating atop the dusting of polystyrene snow, was the most exquisitely-crafted red bus.

For a few, long minutes, she sat there, the decoration dangling from her fingertip as she studied the interior scene, noting the creator had even managed a hint of a driver and passengers within the bus windows, and working her way along, she found the spot where she'd always sat, then the seat she'd found herself in, all the way to the rear of the bus where her journey with Tom had begun.

Leaving the sofa, she crossed to her distressed tree and positioned its new adornment front and centre, before stepping back to admire it, and as she did so, she realised she was grinning. Grinning so widely her face ached and her eyes had squished, and she let out a laugh in a most unusual fashion—because Morgan never laughed without provocation, without a third party with whom to share it, but it was as though Tom stood right there next to her in spirit, and Morgan realised she so very much would like to have him there in person again.

After fetching her mobile from her coat pocket, Morgan paused before the framed photograph of Philip, pressed a finger from her own lips to his. "You'd have liked him—he's a good guy," she said, before glancing at the napkin from the bakery and dialling the number.

Then, pressing the phone to her ear, she waited.

One ring.

Two.

Three.

It took her until the fourth ring to hear the slight echo of the sound. And until the fifth ring for the call to connect.

"Hello?"

Lips parted, she lifted her gaze toward the door through which she'd heard the word almost as clearly as she had through her phone. Then, after hesitating only a second longer, she stepped across the room, lifted her hand to the knob and twisted, and pulled open the barrier to reveal someone she really hadn't expected to see.

Wanted to see, one-hundred-percent yes, but expected?

"Thank you for the gift," she said on a rush of breath.

Tom grinned from beneath the flop of hair even his beanie couldn't contain. "Do you like it?"

"I love it," she said, then realising she spoke into the mouthpiece of her mobile, she lowered the device and found herself grinning up at everything she'd needed to top off a great day. "Hi."

"Hi." Lowering his own phone, he took a step forward, tucking it into his pocket as he leaned slightly against the frame of the door and glanced down her entire body. "Interesting outfit."

She almost cringed in her seasonal dress and bright tights, but instead dropped a half-curtsey. "You like?"

"Strangely, yes." His eyes lingered on her dips and curves for a moment before returning to her face and the blush she could already feel forming there. "Did you have a good time at your gran's?"

"Yes, thank you, I did."

"Good." He stared down at her a moment, his eyes seeming to assess everything about her in a single swoop. "Did you ... you know—*mind* me stopping by?" He half-shrugged. "I mean—"

"No." She waggled her phone. "I was just about to ask you, actually, if you'd like ..."

"To come over?"

"Yes," she said, finding herself caught in his warm gaze.

"Yes," he said back to her. "I really would."

A small giggle escaped her, and she had to resist the urge to smother it with her hand. Because Morgan didn't giggle —at least she hadn't for too long a time. "Maybe you should come in, then."

"Maybe you should let me in, then."

So she did, swinging her body back and to the side to allow him to pass her, before closing the door on the world outside. "It's probably for the best that you came, anyway," she said, as he unzipped his coat and slid it from his shoulders like he'd already hit the comfortable stage of being in her home.

"Yeah?"

"Well, I'd never be able to decide on my own where to put my new ornament on the tree."

"Definitely best that I dropped by, then." He glanced around the room, his gaze landing straight on the blasted article. "Except …"

"Oh, that spot was just a trial run," she said, sweeping across the room and tugging the bauble free of its branch. "Just to *see* if it could go there."

"And it can't?"

"I might need some help deciding." She held up her finger, the delicate glass orb dangling from its tip, and Tom stepped closer to work it lose.

For a moment, he turned to the tree, his head canted to the side like he couldn't study their options straight on. After a few *hums* of consideration, he hung it on a branch not quite centre, and not too low, but in a just-so spot that allowed it to be seen like the centrepiece it was. "There?"

"Perfect."

He turned toward her. "Agreed." But Morgan couldn't be wholly sure he referred to the bauble with that comment, as his eyes deepened with a heat she thought she might actually, if they spent much more time together, be willing to explore.

Just as he had the evening before, he ducked his face in gently, until his lips brushed over hers, but instead of pulling back that time, he lingered, the gentle brush of his tongue adding a hint of spice to his sweetness. And yes, she was totally, without doubt, glad that Tom had stopped by. That she'd had the courage to pick up the phone to call him, even though she hadn't needed to. That she'd been her usual, persevering self and pushed herself toward him, so she'd got to see how much nicer he was than his first impression had allowed.

"Merry Christmas, Morgan King," he murmured, his nose brushing hers.

"Merry Christmas, Tom Michaels" she said.

And for the first time in a long time, she actually meant the words.

※

THANK YOU FOR READING
Reviews are like gold dust to authors.
Please consider leaving a review.
♥

ACKNOWLEDGMENTS

Okay, here goes.

A lot of people actually go into the making of a book, even when it sometimes feel like a very solo venture.

I'd had the idea for this cute Christmassy story a good while back. When I got accepted into the *Light In The Dark* anthology and realised the story *could* fit so well in that if only it wasn't a seasonal tale, I shortened and adapted the story to be included. I wasn't 100% sure at the time if it would even become what I'd originally planned for it, but after a fair bit of struggle with changing my mindset from one story and length to what you have read today, I finally got it done. And I'm so glad I did.

But that wasn't enough. Because I wanted—no, *needed*—the perfect cover to suit it. And a story like this doesn't find its perfect cover just anywhere. No, it needs just the right kind of cover designer to understand the convoluted (and pretty vague) explanation I offered up, and then turn it into something I instantly fell in love with. So this big thanks goes to Shower of Schmidt Designs. You rock!

I'd also like to thank Mr B. He's always on my list, because I'm always at the top of his. He makes sure I'm able to write. And supports me in whatever I do, no matter the odds or opinions of others. And for that, I will be always and forever thankful.

Next up is those of you who read this when it was a completely different version and titled simply *The Night Bus*. Thank you for reading it. Thank you for loving it. You are one of the reasons I pushed forward in making this something *more*.

And of course, I feel here the need to mention TikTok. Last year, I hated the idea of TikTok. Didn't get the hype. Didn't understand how anyone could show their face on there, acting daft and looking so damned relaxed about it all. Didn't get why people viewed and liked the clips they did (still don't understand this). But this year, I took the plunge and gave it a go, and … I bloody love the place now. There is no other platform out there that makes me feel as though I can fully *see* the readers of the world.

Yes, I ***see* you,** BookTokers! And I thank you!

And my last thanks goes, as always, to you! The reader! Without folks like your good self, taking chances on authors and checking out what we have to offer, there would be no authors. You are our anchors in this publishing storm.

ABOUT THE AUTHOR

Best known for her Holloway Pack Stories and The Therapist, J.A. Belfield lives in Solihull, England, with her family, a spoiled dog, and a cat who likes to vomit in unfortunate places.

Once upon a time, she was a little girl with a vivid imagination. Not much has changed in the last forty years.

J.A. Belfield writes paranormal romance, with a second love for urban fantasy. And now she writes saucy and sweet romance, too. Because she can. ;)

COMING 2023

What do you do when in search of Mr. Right? Blog about it, of course.

Well, maybe not a normal person, but Brea McNorty, author of *The Dating Slush Pile* has never claimed to be one of those. Besides, her audience love hearing about her exploits, if only so their own dating disasters don't sound so bad, so why wouldn't she share just how much of a state her love life is in?

After a few years of too many Mr Wrongs ending up on the reject list, Brea's ready to try something new, and the sandy beaches and suggested Happy Ever Afters in the SingleMingle brochure are just too tempting to ignore. When her friend Carrie suddenly announces she's ditching their planned escapade, however, Brea is left with an opening she needs to fill. Or risk going alone.

Milton Lee is the perfect flatmate for Brea. Protective. Unassuming. Always on time with the rent. And the fact he's a bit too comfy walking around in his underwear is merely an added quirk Brea is all too happy to tolerate. On a totally platonic level, of course.

On top of that, the duo just seem to gel, so when Milton offers to step into Carrie's vacated shoes and ensure Brea isn't left to holiday alone, she's only too happy to accept. Especially as he's shadowed all her recent date nights and made sure she's gotten home safe. Stands to reason he's the perfect candidate to do that in sunny Greece, too.

But maybe Brea is looking a little too hard for love. And in all the wrong places. Maybe the possibility of love has been right under her nose—or *roof*—this entire time.

Printed in Great Britain
by Amazon

Morgan King had everything she'd needed. Until one dreadful night when a significant piece of it was cruelly ripped away.

Two years on, she really should've been over the pain and turmoil that threw her life into a blender like a heartbreak milkshake. And she was. Really. What she'd never gotten over, though, was the change. To her life. To her soul. To the very air through which she moved.

The night bus had become her salvation—with a regular driver who knew her quirks and desolations. A distraction from everything that wouldn't allow her to sleep. Although Morgan had found the deterrence to her thoughts by accident, it was one she'd happily repeat for as long as she needed.

She just didn't bank on dealing with one. More. Change.

The driver.

When she finds herself confronted by someone who isn't the guy who's helped her the past couple of years, Morgan is once more filled with an uncertainty she has to process. Least of all because she actually likes the new driver. Thinks of him even once she's tucked beneath the covers and should be sleeping. And Morgan hasn't thought of another man like this since losing the one she loved ...

CAN THE MAGIC OF CHRISTMAS FINALLY WEAVE A SPELL AROUND HER TROUBLED HEART?

THE
Night Bus
BEFORE CHRISTMAS

ISBN 9781838085377